Window Eyes

Kellan Savoy is the creator of over twenty comic book series and graphic novels, including the critically acclaimed *Cupcakes* and *Maze on Dixon.* He is originally from Indiana.

"Working eccentrically in a medium that, as he himself put it, makes eccentricity more tolerable by juvenilizing it, [Kellan] has made available to his readers the greasy, deep ephemera of his psyche, his philosophical self, his faith-wandering self. One is, for instance, able to read him as someone curious about the nature of spirit, someone who, though he does not question the soul's existence, is deeply concerned with why it would choose to seek harbor in the body vessel, a vessel he referred to in his graphic novel *I, Angel*, about an angel who becomes curious about the taste of human flesh, as "a gross constellation of meats and juices." Just the same, one can see his obsession with social contusion, the bruising of the personal narrative through inescapable contact with discompassionate external narratives, a theme central to both *Maze on Dixon* and *Cupcakes* but found in what can be considered its most mature form in the graphic novel *Punching Bag*, one of his more obscure works (with a print run of less than eight hundred) about a boxer in his mid-thirties who, as his mediocre career is winding down, can only find work as a paid-to-be-docile sparring partner for up-and-coming talent. And so too on display are his thoughts on the following and more: technology (*Tramplemundus*, *The Digit*), economics (*Maze on Dixon*, *Crustacean Wedding*, *Blackfoot*), politics (*Maze on Dixon*, *The Mall Beasts*,

Tramplemundus), childhood (*Clothespins and Circuses, The Mall Beasts*), food (*Cupcakes, Windmill Betty, Brine Comedy, I, Angel*), dreams (*Clothespins and Circuses, Blackfoot, The Digit*), good and evil (*Maze on Dixon, The Mall Beasts, Ratio of Sanity*).

But for all the access we have through Kellan's canon to the fibers of his intellect, a truly careful reader will note just how much is left unsaid about the particulars of his heart, not the general demeanor of it, which is clearly filled with some amount of compassion for the human condition, but the personal nature of it, the realm of its private name. His undeniable creative fearlessness has produced panel after panel of raw and unashamedly honest material, material that is often uncomfortable to consume (one of his fans once told him during a Q&A session at the San Diego Comic-Con that reading his work was like reading her mother's diary), and yet, in so many ways, there is something guarded about these same works, something always being avoided, an absence of what one might call the too familiar, the appreciably common, the innocuous out-of-control-ness of the ordinary moment, i.e. the undramatic spaces of life in which the true vulnerability of the human condition has the most wing. Nowhere in his work do we ever see, for instance, a person having breakfast in the absence of some defamiliarizing context like the presence of a mythological creature or an impending catastrophe. Nor do we see a person at rest on a park bench or the changing of a burned-out lightbulb, things through which the delicate personal self can express its unadorned sensitivity. While these are not things that often appear in the extremely limited number of pages found in most comic books, what is hard to ignore is the unusual way that Kellan's work, in contrast to most other comic books (which tend to avoid entirely the need for replacing lightbulbs), approaches these sorts of moments, the way in which his characters and plot trajectories always seem to be accelerating towards them only to veer at the last possible moment away from them and into some extraordinary rendition. As we watch the man on the plane turn away from the passenger with whom he had, prior to the engine failure, been talking about the weather and then calmly begin to eat the unappetizing breakfast on the tray table in front of him, we are struck by a longing for the moment to have completed itself without the catastrophic interruption, just as, one comes to suspect, Kellan himself longed to be able to complete it in that way; that, in general, he has longed for two decades to be able to imagine to completion a place in his worlds for the expression of the unbespoke heart-half of his being, a place where his full self could reside, completedly, in peace."

Preface to this Edition

There are some who have questioned the appropriateness of publishing this work. Given what has happened, we understand their reservations. Nonetheless, we remain resolved.

When asked once in an interview why someone with such strong reclusive tendencies would choose something so public as being an artist, Kellan said the following: "Artistic transmission has the power to transmute the personal into the universal. It is necessary for the evolution of the human spirit. It is the mechanism through which physical and intellectual culture is elevated from collective unconsciousness to collective consciousness. Without it, everything we create, every house, every piece of technology, every politician, is a prison, incarcerating us inside ourselves. The decision to share my work has therefore always been the choice between completion and being alone, between love and death."

It is in the spirit of this philosophy that our decision was made and continues to be executed without regret.

Sincerely,

E.D.

INTRODUCTION

BY THOMAS LEVI

I've known Kellan Savoy for more than thirty years. We grew up together in the small suburban oasis of Shackstown, Indiana. I was, in our childhoods, the fat, clumsy extrovert to his frail glass boy, his corner-sitting boy. We met halfway through the first grade when our teacher, frustrated by my distracting hyper-antics and his refusal to speak to her even if asked a question directly, sat us next to each other in the back of the classroom thinking, I assume, that we would somehow cancel each other out of her perceptions.

Though we would become close, I hated him at first, not for any rational reason but because my six-year-old self saw him as an embodiment of my condemnation, both a reminder of my unwantedness and a punishment for it. Plus, he seemed immune to my efforts to torment him (though as I look back on it as his lifelong friend, to whom he has never spoken of those early moments, he clearly wasn't). He sat at his desk unnervingly still (as he would even as an adult) and was also irritatingly unresponsive (and sometimes was this as an adult as well), wouldn't even talk to me when I asked him questions, although the questions I asked were mostly malicious in nature, and when they weren't outright malicious, they were setups for something malicious, a fact that was obvious to Kellan, who even back then was uncommonly sensitive to the disguised vibrations of human interaction, which, he would eventually explain to me, was why he never answered the questions the teacher asked either: he could tell that she was asking for bureaucratic purposes, that her questions lacked the sincere curiosity that makes questions valuable as opposed to vacant.

Eventually, I wore him down, or he wore me down, or we wore each other down; the silence we sat in together came to belong to us mutually. It developed, after a few weeks, a certain shared quality, the cohesion of a zip code, and so, one day when some of the other kids tried to take Kellan's lunch from him in the schoolyard, I instinctively walked up to their leader and pushed him to the ground. I didn't intend it as such, but that was the first moment of our friendship, the moment when Kellan welcomed me into his world, an ordinarily not insignificant gesture, this welcoming of one person into another, but in Kellan's case, an exaggerated experience. Not only did he start to talk to me (and only me), he also shared with me his drawings and some of the vocabulary of his head, the unique vocabulary of symbols and concepts that he used to shape the world into his own personal reality. In fact, he had a dictionary of these concepts, a sort of visual diary that he kept. On that first day, after we returned from recess, he tore a page out of that diary and gave it to me, a page on which he had drawn what I believe is his base symbolic understanding of friendship: a small boy sharing a cupcake with a dragon.

I have hundreds of those pages now, accumulated over the first ten years of our friendship. Kellan used to give them to me at crucial emotional junctures like when his grandmother, the only other person he spoke to regularly, died or when he got his first crush on a girl. I think it became his way of processing his emotions, of collecting the nauseating swirl of them in one place, and then letting them go. I keep these pages in the same shoebox my mother put the first dozen in when she found them lying carelessly around my room, after I explained to her what they were. I take them out sometimes, at my own emotional junctures, and manipulate them like a puzzle or like those little magnetic words that people put on their refrigerators. I organize them into different configurations, and though I don't quite know why, somehow it soothes me, helps me to understand the world better. This, it seems to me, is the appeal of Kellan's work in general: how, almost magically, the weird gestures and symbols that he employs have a strange, counterintuitive way of making the cumbersome gestures and symbols of the world that we all live in seem clearer to us. It is almost anti-marketing in nature, the way that what it cryptically broadcasts makes us feel less alone, less bad about who we are, less in need of something to make ourselves feel whole.

Throughout his life, Kellan was told by therapists, family members and others that he was too disconnected from his feelings; that he was robotic, stunted, and while I agree that his work certainly tended toward emotional guardedness, the impact that his work has on *our* emotional states, its ability to clarify our inner worlds to some degree, speaks to the difficulty that exists in truly being able to translate through conventional methods his unique experiences into something that the rest of us are able to find correlates for in our own universes; it speaks, perhaps, to the limits we have placed on what it means to be human, to a secret universality that comes in above or below our intellectual radar. It is clear to me as his friend of thirty years that Kellan's real struggle in his personal life has been with the imposition of these limits on his self-hood. The production of his first comic at sixteen (one of only two that has never seen publication, the only one that I have never seen but which I am nonetheless certain exists since Kellan is not one for deception, not even a terrible liar, just someone who never even tries to lie) coincides with the end of the dictionary he kept (and consequently the end of my receiving pages from him, from that dictionary), and where I have believed for some time that his comics evolved out of and are an extension of the mechanism he had for dealing with the emotional chaos inside him, more and more, I have come to suspect that the transition from that early dictionary of sketches to the comic medium represents the moment when he first began to formulate a true awareness of this struggle. I speculate that it was the end of his pubescence, the birth of his adulthood, the moment when he began, without necessarily realizing it directly, to contemplate his own loneliness.

And I think then that he began to contemplate the end to his loneliness eighteen years later with *D.ynamo O.pera S.ynergy* and the graphic novel *Blackfoot*, the last two works he published before his disappearance. These two works were panned by critics and fans alike as being flaccid and gelatinous, but at a recent comic symposium, Martha Villanova, creator of the best-selling-comic-turned-hit-TV show *Awful Wednesdays* and Kellan's longtime rival, offered a defense of them, suggesting that the problem was not with the work but with the fans, who had become overly enamored with what she referred to as "the spectacle of their own hopelessness", which Kellan had, for most of his career, "consumed and fed back to them, articulated, adorned and beautiful." They were, according to her, judging Kellan's recent efforts based not on the merit of those works but on their inability to relinquish the sainted mediocrity of their own lives. She went on to say that anyone who looked at these works with honest eyes, absent any investment in a particular reality, would see that, though they remained at least somewhat guarded in the way that Kellan's works had always been guarded, they moved quite noticeably toward something, "the folding back of certain petals*," so that by the time one had read from the beginning of *D.O.S.*'s twelve issues through to the end of the subsequently published sixty-four pages of the graphic novel *Blackfoot*, one felt certain that Kellan's next work, whatever it would be, would reveal a secret that was not new, but which, as was suddenly clear, all his previous works had been preluding to.

I certainly remember, upon reading these works myself, as Kellan was creating them, not only thinking something similar, but being surprised by what seemed to be the emergence of parts of Kellan that after more than a quarter century of knowing him, I hadn't realized were there. Natalie Serrano's appearance in Kellan's life had prompted an awakening of something in him that had within the range of its endeavors a capacity for celebrating life. For as long as I had known him, I had thought him devoid or uninterested in such capacity. He seemed to me to be an unredeemable reticent, someone curious about the world but afraid to touch or be touched by the things he was curious about. I, like his chief critic Jeremy Stronk, had, in fact, understood the Overseer in *The Digit*, the mysterious, never seen entity conducting the experiments on the book's main character, the man known only as 1, to be a projection or encapsulation of this strong aspect of his persona. Then in *D.O.S.* we suddenly encounter Lushly, the impish child-spirit with Cupidian powers, a character unlike any other character in Kellan's previous works, precocious and heartwarmingly comical. Lushly's existence ignites a reevaluation through which one comes to realize that the Overseer had been all along a caricature, a dark spoofing of an aspect of himself that Kellan had apparently been for all those years yearning to overcome.

Even as his closest friend, I hadn't realized Kellan was capable of such self-satirization or—and for this I feel absolutely foolish in retrospect—that he, like the rest of us, could be changed so radically by love. While he was clearly uncomfortable with other people, I had become convinced that he was comfortable being who he was in ways that I, being host to primarily unremarkable qualities, never could be comfortable with myself. Given the subject of *Blackfoot*, a man desperately seeking atonement for having stepped on a young flower, there is reason to believe that Kellan himself had been convinced of this also. He came across to all those who knew him as someone strengthened by his isolation from the normalizing habits the average person uses to exchange creative potential for companionship, and most of us, as far as I know, admired him for this (it's the primary reason that I, if not the others as well, tolerated his sometimes alienating behaviors). We admired him and, more than that, took pleasure, as his fans had, in watching him traverse territories that we were all too afraid to explore on our own. If I'm being completely honest, certain aspects of loving Kellan had become fetishized over the years–I, for one, certainly depended on the excitement I would feel whenever Kellan produced a work that transgressed normative boundaries–which no doubt played a role in how we were ultimately surprised by Natalie's impact on him.

Perhaps the only person not surprised was Natalie herself, who seemed from the start to see a Kellan that no one else knew. She was also an artist, a painter hired by Kellan's publisher High Mind to paint a portrait of Kellan for a promotion they'd orchestrated. The portrait she produced (the first of several, though the only one produced under contract for High Mind) captured an ephemeral lightness of being and subtle, unconditioned cheeriness that High Mind, wanting a rendition highlighting the unique melancholic brooding quality that Kellan's fans and critics loved so much, considered unfaithful to their vision (they never used the portrait, and if memory serves me, never paid Natalie, who refused their request to repaint). Kellan was also upset by the portrait, for entirely different reasons than his publisher; though I am certain he could not express or even understand what the reasons actually were, and the reasons he could and did express to me on the phone before confronting Natalie directly were half-cooked and fireworkish, full of pow, flaky shimmer and nothing else.

At the time this occurred, Kellan was working on the final issue of *Ratio of Sanity*, the published version of which includes, in the penultimate scene, a moment where the main character, Otello, questions the reality of a mirror he stands naked in front of. Knowing that the reflection, no matter what the case might be, has no substance, Otello concerns himself only with the possibility that he is hallucinating the mirror itself. He ultimately resorts to violence, thrusting his fist into the mirror glass and lacerating his knuckles. In all versions of this issue, there is a panel featuring Otello's bloody hand resting on a marble sundial, but prior to the unveiling of Natalie's portrait, Otello cut his hand on the teeth of the priest to whom he had come to confess a list of sins that he'd invented to express the unassignable guilt he always felt. Kellan made the changes after returning from his confrontation with Natalie, in the month that followed it, during which time he worked on nothing else. In all the years that I had been reading his works-in-progress, I had never seen him revise something so profoundly, or have so much difficulty with a revision, and it is clear to me now, having knowledge of where his work would go from there, that what seemed to me at the time to be a series of creative temper tantrums were in fact the throes of a metamorphosis. The external revision of those panels was an extension of a significant shifting of his internal world, a reconfiguring necessary for him to make sense of the problem that Natalie had unwittingly presented him with: how to account for this sudden desire he felt to accommodate the world of another within his own. I imagine that something similar had occurred within him all those years earlier in the first grade when he decided to share his world with someone outside it, but where that, a minor trauma requiring only the addition of an outlet to his world, risked minimal contamination, this required the unthinkable: for him to embrace contamination itself as a way forward.

In the year before he disappeared, I only saw Kellan a handful of times. He became a shut-in after the accident, even more so than he'd been beforehand. I tried to visit him at least once a week, but he usually turned me away or ignored my entreaties entirely. When he did allow me into his home, he seemed unusually territorial, confining me aggressively to the same small corner of his living room each time.

Almost every one of those few successful visits ended in the same way: he threw me out when I asked him if he was working on anything new. Presumably, Kellan was working on *Window Eyes*—what is, as of this writing, as far as anyone knows, the last of his completed works—but it was a project he wasn't ready to share with anyone. Its creation must have been a profoundly personal experience for him, like the shedding of some internal part of himself, the expulsion of a sack of emotional organs that he no longer had any use for, and at that point, he was still too raw.

Of course, I am only able to speculate. *Window Eyes* is the only work of Kellan's—besides that first comic of his— that was completed in total solitude, without the input of outside parties such as me or his editor, Egret, without even the quiet, feedbackless consumption that Kellan often requests of us where his works-in-progress are concerned. What little I know of its creation, I have gathered circumstantially from conversations with the few people who had contact with him while he was making it. I know, for instance, from his mother, whom Kellan allowed into his apartment barely more than myself but whom he permitted on a few evenings to sleep there, that he, to her recollection, worked deep into the night, which means that *Window Eyes*, owing to Kellan's inflexible artistic insistence on working in the natural light of the sun, from which he had never before diverged, is the only work of his infused with what he referred to in his work *Tramplemundus* as "mortal photons." I know also, from Sally, who used to walk Kellan's dog Metro before Metro died, the only person that Kellan, in this year of almost total seclusion, would leave his house with, that he, who had been fascinated since he was a teenager by the highly codified process of Hebrew Torah manufacture, would, as the Torah scribes do, bury, in the park, any pages he deemed unredeemable. And I know from Reinhart, a professor friend of his, that during this period, Kellan consumed over one hundred obscure books on the subject of Cartography, books which Reinhart, owing to the age of most of them, went to great lengths to procure for him.

What there is to say of the work itself will be largely left to the following pages, but certain things do bear mentioning here. First: I believe, based upon something I also learned from Sally plus my own handling of it, that it was composed entirely on parchment made from animal skin, another technique borrowed from Torah manufacture. This impacted the art itself, particularly the colorings, which, though less visibly vibrant, obtained from the oils in the skins an appealing organic luster that is impossible using paper made from trees.

Second: while the work bears the hallmarks of Kellan's unique consciousness, it differs qualitatively from what he has produced in the past. It is uneven, sometimes distant and unfocused, coarse and overbearing. While it would be easy to be critical of this, it is important to keep in mind that it is a work created by someone as loss was consuming them, at a time when aesthetic rationality was overcome by psychic torrent and, as such, is raw in a way that wants empathy over judgement; what would otherwise seem to be flaws should instead be given consideration as the public exposure of a deeply personal nerve, a rare and difficult to obtain glimpse into the unabridged mortality of a human being.

Third: what follows is each of *Window Eyes*'s twenty-two-and-a-half, variable-size issues presented in summary. The actual art and text of the work is unavailable, having disappeared with Kellan. All that remains is my memory of having read it on the last night I saw my friend, who, on the eve of his disappearance, had unexpectedly summoned me to his home for the purpose of reading the work in its entirety. Though it is certainly unusual to present so visual a work this way, I and Egret, to whom I recounted the work several months after Kellan's disappearance, believe its power merits this. We both, however, agree that such a transmission is not without its difficulties. To mitigate, I have provided accompanying content[**]. Furthermore, because I am, as the intermediary between the reader and the work, now inextricably part of the experience, Egret has encouraged me to include my own thoughts, not just on the work itself, but also on my friend.

With that, I bid you off on this strange journey. May it bring to you, as it brought to me, the triumvirate of sensations Kellan called "the three-sided face of divinity": wonder, horror, and awe.

T.L.

---

[*] a reference, I think, to the first several panels of *D.ynamo O.pera S.ynergy* which depict in extensive detail the opening of a flower

[**] While you are free to read this work any way that you wish, it is my suggestion that the reader approach the summaries on their own first, ignoring the annotation, to embrace Kellan's vision as much as possible without interruption, and then return to the beginning and read through a second time, inclusive of the notes. Also, those who are already fans of Kellan's work might find some of the information presented in the notes obvious or redundant, but know that this was necessary to make the work as universally accessible as possible.

Window Eyes

by Kellan Savoy

ISSUE 1

OCTOBER[1]

Cover: A grassy field at night. The only objects are the blades of grass and the full moon in the starless sky.

Summary:

A man is taking a bath. The water is clear. The man is wearing a black suit with a white shirt and a black tie. After the bath, he silently wanders the house in his wet suit, visiting various rooms, stopping at one point in the master bedroom where he winds a grandfather clock with an ornate brass key[2,3,4,5].

Eventually, he comes to rest at a desk in a dimly lit study. He puts his elbows on the desk and allows his head to fall forward into his hands. Water falls from him onto the desk[6]. He sits at the desk and sits at the desk and sits at the desk. About a third of the comic, which contains absolutely no speech, is panel after silent panel[7,8] of the man at the desk from what begins as different angles but eventually becomes different perceptions: the first few angles are standard–from the man's left, from his right, from just above the man–but each successive angle after those is increasingly more obscure–from under the desk looking up at the bend in the man's knees, a close-up of the back of one of the man's ears, from the top of his head through his hairs at the edge of the desk and the floor beyond–until the mounting tension of this obscurity snaps and the mode of perception itself shifts to an x-ray rendering of the room (the man's bones and organs are visible as are some of the things contained in the desk's drawers, etc...), to a panel in the style of a caricature that one might commission from a street artist complete with disproportionately large head and exaggerated features (here the most prominent exaggeration is the man's wetness, it is as if the man is interred in a teardrop), to a puzzle-like rendering[9]. Finally, at the bottom right corner of the page, there is a return to standard perception: a bird's eye view of the room from directly over the chair the man is sitting in. The first panel of the next page is identical to this panel except that the man is no longer in it. We can see the pattern that has been formed across the floor and chair and desk by the wet that has sloughed off of him, a Rorschach type image[10]. The entire page is that panel repeated nine times.

On the next page, the man reappears in the room with a shovel. He moves through the room and disappears out a door in the room that leads to the backyard. The images then zoom in one panel at a time toward the desktop, toward the things that sit on it. The final image of the issue is a close-up of the desk, on which sits a picture frame containing the photo of a woman and next to it an invitation to a funeral. The date and location are visible on the invitation, but the name of the deceased is distorted by water that has fallen on it.

Notes

---

[1] Kellan put this date on the front cover in a box that he had drawn to simulate the price/date/logo section of a normal comic. I don't know what the month is supposed to represent. Natalie died in November, and I visited him for the final time in September of the following year, making October the only month he couldn't have worked on this comic. This is the only issue that bears such a date.

[2] The way that Kellan depicts this character's stroll through the house is disorienting. He provides us with no continuity clues. Each panel captures in great detail a space in the house, but none of the panels contain any overlapping information[2a], and so, while it is possible to see what rooms the house contains (or at least some of them) and also what some of the pass-through spaces look like, it is not possible to determine where any of these things are relative to any of the others[2b]. These rooms therefore exist without a relationship to one another, the ultimate effect being that each of them seems to be a space of its own in exile from the rest.

[2a] No item in the house appears in more than one panel.

[2b] The panels visit some of these rooms more than once—a conjecture I am making based on the various items depicted and where one would normally expect to find them in a house—and in a fashion that undermines the reader's ability to infer anything about the house from the way the panels are sequenced; the structure defeats or at least confuses the assumption that we are presented with the panels in an order that reflects the arrangement of the house's internal space.

[3] The lack of relativity affects my ability to recall, in anything close to the detail that Kellan presented them in, the rooms of the house that were depicted in this issue. I know that, in addition to the master bedroom, which had a king-size four-post bed catty-cornered near a window, there was a kitchen with a magnet covered refrigerator (there was a panel that contained a close-up of these magnets, a flock of birds and business cards and famous logos, McDonald's and Amazon and Munduson's, the made up mega-corporation that appeared over and over in Kellan's work, most prominently, of course, in *Tramplemundus,*

a series centered around three superheroes whose alter-egos all work in some bureaucratic capacity for the Munduson Company and slowly, as a result of this employment, lose their desire to use their powers to do good), two almost identical bathrooms distinguished from one another by the color of the bathmats on the floor near the bathtubs (and so at first it seems like he is visiting the same bathroom multiple times), a living room with a gigantic, purple plush couch and large television with a cracked screen, a foyer with a flowerpot in one of the corners near the door, a study with a desk and a fireplace and built-in shelving.

[4] Kellan loved the idea of the house as a metaphor for the mind and would use houses in his work to tour the psyches of various characters, room by room. The most famous example of this comes from *The Mall Beasts*, issue 8, which is just a real estate agent taking a couple on a tour, from the basement to the attic, of the house that Tulip Farache, one of the comic's main characters, is selling.

[5] The house depicted in this issue bears no resemblance to the house that Natalie and Kellan had bought together and lived in for the final year of Natalie's life, but the items contained in many of the scenes have been plucked from that house. Here is an inexhaustive list: the loud grandfather clock that Natalie had bought broken at a pawn shop and then repaired, which in the actual house had been less uncannily placed in the foyer, and the print of Van Gogh's Starry Night, a college dormitory-type print that they had pasted little fragments of their own art to[5a], which had hung in the bedroom over their bed in the real house but was leaning unhung and on its side against a wall in the kitchen of the fictional house, and the rocking horse that Natalie had built so that Kellan, doing research for *Blackfoot*, could observe her building it, which had been in the basement of their home but was sitting obtrusively on the landing where the fictional house's staircase turned at a ninety degree angle, and the geode they'd brought back from their honeymoon in southeastern Utah, the one item that was located in the same relative place in both houses, over the fireplace in the study.

[5a] Kellan went to great lengths to reproduce this exactly, capturing in miniature each of the fragments they had added.

[6] It is unclear whether the water is from the bath or if he is crying[6a].

[6a] Kellan found the experience of crying to be indistinguishable from the experience of being covered in water. According to him, the feeling that produced tears was identical to a sadness he always felt when his face was wet[6b].

[6b] This was one of the things that Kellan told Natalie on their first date, one of those strange details that have a way of slipping out of us when our compatibility with another person is of a certain high degree.

[7] As fans and critics know, the use of silence is one of Kellan's signature moves: lengthy tense pauses, drawing out the silence of a scene[7a]. While he has been doing it since the beginning, he first brought this technique to perfection in *Maze on Dixon*, building the silence between Seraphim and Maryanne a little bit in each episode, starting with what amounted to a small awkward hiccup in the first issue, then a two panel pause in the second issue when Seraphim accidentally knocks his coffee over while gesturing animatedly, etc.… until the final issue in which a single word is exchanged in the first panel followed by thirty-one pages during which the characters sit tensely in a silence embellished with depictions of their subtle fidgets, a silence they carry out into the world with them when they stand up on the last page and leave Maze Coffee.

[7a] Jeremy Stronk has the following to say about these silences: "They are a tool [Kellan] uses not to expose the complications of modern life but to dispose of those complications, to eradicate them from the equation of discovery. It is a form of philosophical nudity that challenges the prudish nature of our illusions, a way to run our sins up the flagpole.[7b]"

[7b] This certainly seems true from Stronk's impersonal vantage point, but I, knowing Kellan as I do, have always believed the silence to be a reflection of the troubles he has had building relationships with others and that, furthermore, much of his work is fundamentally about traversing and/or conquering that silence (and/or the failure to do so, as is sometimes the case). In fact, his characters, in my opinion, exist solely to fill it. He is driven to create them out of need to find the reflections of himself that he cannot find readily in the world[7c].

[7c] Where most of us take for granted the ease with which we find these reflections, for Kellan it is an arduous and sometimes seemingly impossible task. Aside from myself, he has had only a few people firmly in his life: Sharon (his mother, a woman who has struggled

unsuccessfully to understand him and for whom I have a great deal of fondness), Egret (his editor, who has given me permission to produce this book and also to mention her by name), Reinhart (a professor from Kellan's college days who has always struck me as more of an "investigator of" than a "friend to") and Sally (the dog walker who used to walk Kellan's now deceased dog). There was also, of course, Natalie, but for now, let's say Kellan's entire adult life, his entire adult self, has been anchored, and anchored tenuously, to the world outside him by this inelegantly assembled handful. We are a group with almost no connection to each other (myself and Sharon excepted), an unsteady constellation of disparate individuals bonded only by Kellan's decision to allow each of us access to some part of his core[7d].

[7d] What Kellan wants us to be–what we fail over and over again to be simply because we are all approximations, and yet what maybe we are to him in the deepest parts of his mind after his imagination strips away our deficiencies–appears over and over again in his work: the baking class that forms around Darby in *Cupcakes*, the recurring cast of 1's hallucinations in *The Digit*, the party guests that Maryanne describes to Seraphim in *Maze on Dixon*, and, even to a lesser extent, the zoo animal menagerie that the robots gather and dress like people in *A Conspiracy of Slumber*. Almost every one of Kellan's works contains a silence-filling conclave of sorts embodying an ideal, an umbilical congregation between his fetal need for sustenance and the womb of reality[7e].

[7e] But we, the uninvented, his harvested companions, are not that, and so Kellan has difficulties getting what he needs from the people around him[7f].

[7f] He has difficulty sometimes with even the most basic human interaction. In my own experiences, it is not uncommon for Kellan to withdraw inexplicably and without warning during one of our conversations, for him to go almost completely catatonic, or for him to simply fall out of sync with what we are doing, to suddenly stop, for instance, in the middle of carrying a couch up a flight of stairs and begin to tell me a story that he remembered his grandmother telling him when he was a child[7g].

[7g] These difficulties are only amplified when Kellan is forced to interact with people whom he is not bonded with in any way, which is evident

to anyone who has watched his interview on Australian television, the way the entire thing begins to collapse almost from the start, how it collapses in a way that even the host can't prevent, so that by the end, the things that Kellan is saying, his stark recollection of the pornographic dream he'd had the night before (and also the look in the host's eyes as he finds himself inexplicably unable to stop what's happening), upend not just our assessment of his sanity but the collective assessment, co-signed by all of us on an unconscious level, that we, as a species, are sane.

[8] I find the silence here, in this first issue of *Window Eyes*, to be particularly excruciating. It is, from my perspective, different from all the other silences in Kellan's work in that it is a rebounding silence, the return of a silence that I saw Natalie drive at least partially into exile. It recalls for me some of the moments I shared with the two of them, in particular those moments we spent together on the back porch of their house, the moments we spent chatting over the great rattle of the cicadas, the discussions we had about nothing specific, the rhythms we would fall into, rhythms that had once been impossible between Kellan and other people but which suddenly made sense because somehow Natalie's rhythms filled the spaces where Kellan's rhythms had always been broken. And it reminds me of the interior of that house, which I was forced to visit recently on Kellan's behalf, at the request of his mother, a house that has been vacant for close to three years, the vacancy of which has, in that time, grown like the ivy that now covers the house's exterior. The warmth the house had held when last I saw it occupied by Kellan and Natalie has been completely smothered.

[9] Weirdly, the puzzle is complete. None of the pieces are missing. The panel is simply puzzlelated, which raises the question of why bother to render the image in this way? I have been thinking about this since that night, but this remains one of many unanswered questions I have.

[10] That to me looked like a moth whose wings were withering in the presence of an intense source of heat.

ISSUE 2

Cover: The same field as in the first cover, same moon. Now present is a shovel that has been stuck into the earth, standing upright.

Summary:

The man is in his basement, sitting on a stool, surrounded by jars and buckets of dirt. He reaches into one of the buckets and pulls out a pinch of dirt. He examines it in the light, both at a distance and near his eyes. He listens to the sound it makes when he allows a few sprinkles to fall from his hand to the tile floor. He tastes the dirt. Then he mixes a handful of it with water from one of the jars and flings the mixture at one of the walls.

Over the course of several panels, the mud crawls slowly down the wall.

The man examines dirt from another bucket in the same way, then from another. He pauses here to grab a jar from the floor and begins to sob, collecting his tears to the best of his ability in the jar[1]. At the end of the cry, he holds the jar up to examine its contents in the light. This is depicted, over the course of several panels, from the perspective of a photon[2] in a beam of that light: an image of his face, refracted[3] through the jar and liquid inside it, closed in upon over the panels' progression, the sequence terminating inside the liquid, only his eye still visible through the glass. Then, the jar is lowered so that the eye is visible, not unrefracted but now refracted only by the thin layer of liquid the eye has coated itself with. The man spits into the jar several times to increase the amount of liquid in it and puts it back on the floor.

More dirt sampling, two or three more cycles. Finally, the man selects one of the buckets and pours the contents of all the remaining jars into it to make a large quantity of mud. He strips off his clothing and begins to apply the mud to his body until he is covered from head to toe in a layer. Then he lies down on the floor and curls into a fetal position. The last few panels depict the area of the basement where the wall that the man has been flinging the mud at meets the floor. A clump of mud on the wall slides into the small pile that has formed on the tiling.[4]

Notes

---

[1] This action was difficult to make out at first. Kellan seemed to have trouble envisioning the proper angle, both physically and conceptually, for portraying it on account of it possessing a high "coefficient of unfamiliarity[1a]", which, according to him, is the force that an artist must overcome when the object they are rendering has no common correlate in the reality that the art's viewer is coming from[1b].

[1a] As far as I know, this is a term he came up with.

[1b] Here's my understanding of Kellan's theory: When rendering something like a car, an object that people see often, the coefficient is low, so the artist can draw almost anything that resembles, even remotely, a car, and people will know what it is. The same would be true for a baseball player taking a swing at a baseball. But in the case of a man crying into a jar, an object having effectively no correlate for viewers (the one or two people who have cried into a jar or seen someone do it are meaningless here), the artist must not only render the object accurately, but they must also overcome the viewer's resistance to change. Another way to put it would be to say that the artist, in addition to giving the viewer enough information to understand what the object is, must also provide enough reason for the viewer to willingly expand their ongoing dialogue with reality[1c].

[1c] Because this was something Kellan generally excelled at (take, for example, the clarity with which he portrayed Otello extracting the soul of a starfish in *Ratio of Sanity*), his challenge in rendering this scene likely stems from something outside of his artistic ability.

[2] I know that Kellan, before Natalie's death, had planned a series about a photon that had passed through the exact moment when two aliens from a faraway galaxy first realized their love for each other. He intended to explore the journey of the photon as it carries this moment across the entire universe for billions of years, eventually arriving on Earth where it is absorbed into a bowl of tomato soup, elevating the complexity and temperature of the soup in its miniscule way right before the soup is consumed by a lonely earthling.

[3] Kellan became obsessed with refraction when we learned about it in a middle school physics class. He spent the next several years reading every physics and architecture textbook he could find on the subject. When I asked him why he found it so interesting, he explained to me that as far as he could tell, all experience was refracted; that everything that happens is refracted before we are able to say that it has happened to us; that we somehow refract everything that happens so that it seems like it is happening to us. This made him sad and so he had undertaken to understand the mechanisms of refraction in hopes that he could better recognize his own refractive processes and eventually stop them. He wanted badly to see the unrefracted world, the world that Seraphim describes to Maryanne in issue six of *Maze on Dixon* ("the Unindentured World" in which "every molecule in the universe is peacefully apolitical"). Eventually, he stopped obsessing over the subject, but it has remained a constant theme in nearly all his works.

[4] The emotional content of this issue is heightened through the coloring (unique from the other issues, which conform to an established standard), the exclusive three or four tones, the reds, browns, grays, whites that Kellan selected to work with. Also, Kellan opted not to ink this issue, so all the pencil lines are buried beneath the colors, creating a world without solid, enunciated boundaries. The man, the buckets and the basement all exist as part of a single field of objects bleeding into one another. The word to describe this would be muddy, which, if I know Kellan, was not an accident. He loved this sort of "word play" and would often incorporate it into his art. He took great pleasure in evoking descriptions of his work that were painfully on the nose[4a].

[4a] Natalie also loved this aspect of his work, and Kellan loved that she recognized what he was doing without having to be told. It is no surprise that this "word play" occurs more frequently in *D.O.S.* and *Blackfoot.*

ISSUE 3

Cover: The same field as in the first and second cover, same moon. The top half of the shovel juts out from the grassline, suggesting a hole. Now present is a mound of dirt to the right of the shovel.

Summary:

The man has set up a table in his basement. He sits on a stool in front of the table with his back to the reader. A bucket rests on the floor near his left calf. Over the course of a few panels, we can see that the man's arms are moving, that he is doing something on the table, but his body hides his hands and their actions[1]. As he works, the man is speaking. He seems to be reciting a list of items[2] that could be found in a grocery store[3]. Each panel contains the naming of a single item[4]. In the second-to-last panel of this sequence, the man says, "fresh lemons." In the final panel he says, "But they didn't have any of those today."

On the next page, the angle shifts. We see a close-up of the top half of the man's face, from the center of the bridge of his nose to just under his hairline. The focus is on the eyes. The pupils are extremely dilated and surrounded by a rim of blue that is rippled throughout with golden hazel streaks[5]. In the corneas, it is possible—but only after deliberate inspection—to make out the faint image of a face[6,7].

A return to a more comprehensive perspective. The man continues to speak[8]: "I have not had a decent fresh lemon in a long time. My memory of what they taste like is starting to break down at the edges. It bleeds into other memories. I find myself thinking about the lemon bars my mother used to pack in my brown bag lunches, but what I want to be thinking about is the way that fresh lemons curdle the tastebuds." In front of him, on a banding wheel, is a head made from thick, plasticitous mud, seen only from behind[9]. The man continues to talk about lemons, and what began with his memories becomes a discourse on the history of lemons[10] that traces the origins of the lemon backwards through time from the man's first encounter with a lemon all the way to the big bang. The sequence takes place across several pages consisting of panels that depict him at work on the head, which head we continue to see only from behind. In these panels, the man's torso remains steady. The illusion of motion is carried out through his head and hands and arms. Each panel captures these three elements in a unique relation to one another[11]. Each panel also contains a unique arrangement of clay[12] bits sailing through the air off the head.

As the history of lemons comes to a conclusion, at the exact point when, in the story of the universe, everything becomes nebulous, the man stops what he is doing. He picks up the head off the table and brings it close to his face. We are suddenly presented with a close-up of the head's front side. The face is only two lips, immaculately carved from the clay[13], and a small galaxy-shaped mark[14] imprinted on the left cheekbone's apex[15]. The man kisses the face on the lips, puts it back on the stand and then returns to work. In the last few panels, we view things again from behind the

head. The man works as he did before. Pieces of clay fly
through the air.

Notes

---

[1] For a moment, I thought he was changing a baby's diaper, such was the nature of the motions[1a].

[1a] I couldn't account for where the baby had come from, but having long since become accustomed to the two most prominent settings for Kellan's work, surreal realities and banal realities in which the revelation of information is manipulated so that a world functioning ordinarily appears surreal, my confusion was unabated by reason. It seemed possible to me that the baby had either appeared out of nowhere to serve some purpose that Kellan would eventually reveal or that the man had been a father this entire time and Kellan had been intentionally presenting us with glimpses of the man at times when the baby was unavailable (so maybe the scene in the last issue, I thought, had taken place while the baby was being babysat at his/her grandparents' house).

[2] The first words attributed to him in the entire series are "an uncut pineapple", though as written, it was preceded by an ellipsis: "…an uncut pineapple".

[3] Admittedly, this is a conclusion I came to after the fact.

[4] The impression that I got here was that each word accompanied a single unit of whatever thing his arms and hands were doing.

[5] In the previous issue, owing to the limited color scheme (or really the muddying of the entire world) (or so I believe), the man's eyes were brown.

[6] Kellan rendered this effect with so much care, so faithfully, that I initially thought, before inspecting the faint face more closely, that I was seeing a reflection of my own self in the oily sheen of the parchment[6a]. Upon closer inspection, it was clear to me that the face belonged to a woman that reminded me of Natalie but was not Natalie. Kellan had carefully laid her over the iris areas of the protagonist's eyes. She appears there like a ghost. Upon realizing this, I was embarrassed, because of the likeness to Natalie, to have mistaken her for myself, even in the slight way that I had.

[6a] At the time of this mistake, I had not yet noticed that the image was found in both of the eyes. I saw it only in the left eye and was drawn to

it as one is generally drawn to what they believe to be an unexpected reflection of themselves.

[7] The face is crafted with remarkable detail. I had access to a pair of reading glasses that Kellan's mother had recently left at his place and used them to inspect the image. Kellan had managed to capture the face on the page with the clarity that the cornea of the eye is able to capture a face in its reflective surface. He also managed to capture the translucence. You could see through the face, through the high cheekbones and thin pink lips and light brown of its eyes, to the iris behind it[7a].

[7a] I have wondered over these months whether or not this effect would have been publishable, if perhaps it was something too delicate to be reproduced by machines. When I suppose that yes, a machine could have technically reproduced it, I wonder if the enormous care and effort that Kellan had put into this, the days he had most likely spent on just these tiny images, would be lost in the translations, eaten up by the emotionless way the machines pushed the inks into the pages, numbed out by the mindless replication. I know that Kellan had to have thought of these things. He is always concerned about the impact that technology has on his work. He is concerned, in general, about how we live in a world where, without us truly knowing it, we are communicating most of the time with machines; that rarely do we ever connect directly with other humans anymore[7b] (the irony of him saying this was, as many ironies were, lost on him). Telephones, he likes to tell me (quite often for such an esoteric fact), break down our voices and words into streams of digits and then reconstruct those streams of digits into sound at the other end, which means that it is technically the phone itself talking to us, which means that technically the phone is impersonating us. And the same is true with text messages and emails: even if the thought originates with us, it is the phone or computer that is sharing it with the other person. And that where comics are concerned, if the machines are doing all the printing, the art that we see is art produced by them, even if that art is the machines' plagiarization of something human made.

[7b] He addresses these concerns most directly in *The Digit,* his seminal series in which a man with amnesia who is trapped in a laboratory is

endlessly exposed to machine-generated reports containing scientific data that some mysterious observer or observers is/are constantly gathering about him, and *A Conspiracy of Slumber*, a series that follows several AI entities as they explore their idyllic machine world and reflect on the lethargy that led to the decline and non-violent extinction of their human creators. There is a sequence in particular from *The Digit*, beginning in issue number seven, in which the man, known only as 1, having not seen an actual person or even a reflection of himself in a mirror since returning to consciousness without memory, comes to believe that some of the machines in the room with him must be other people and gives them names. Several issues later, when an event jars loose some chunk of his suppressed prior self, he begins to hallucinate other humans and ultimately must determine whether it is the machines or the hallucinations who are more like him and thus his true companions.

[8] The text is contained in dialogue bubbles located in the margins (which are wider here than is standard, likely so they can host what's being said). The bubbles are connected to their panels by fine strings of ink.

[9] This view of the head mirrors the view we had of the man's head a few panels earlier.

[10] There is a quality to this reminiscent of a malfunction. Fans of Kellan have seen this before in *Brine Comedy*, his "kitchen comic," which follows the life of a chef slowly driven mad by the pursuit of a flavor that she is certain she has experienced before but cannot name. The chef, Verunica, at one point, during meal prep, begins to chant the history of the potato as the kitchen staff struggle around her to prepare the complex menu she has concocted for a dinner party honoring the ambassador of Portugal[10a].

[10a] While Kellan, like any artist, repeats certain themes in his work, he has never before reused any ideas. I am left to question whether or not Kellan himself was suffering a sort of malfunction as he created this issue, one in which he found himself unable to distinguish between the creative present and the creative past[10b].

[10b] What interests me most here is that the issue of *Brine Comedy* with the potato incident was the first issue that High Mind published after

Anthony Wentz took over as High Mind's head of marketing[10c]. Anthony was the individual who hired Natalie to paint Kellan's portrait.

[10c] I remember this because Anthony called Kellan after reading that issue to offer Kellan some "advice" that Kellan had not asked for, and I, in turn, had to listen, for hours, to Kellan's "thoughts" on this intrusion.

[11] I do not remember the exact configurations, but for the sake of clarity by way of example, let's say that in the first of these panels the man's left hand, his left arm bent at a right angle, grips the top of the clay head while the right hand holds a cutting tool at eye level, the tip of it angled toward his temple by the bend in the right elbow, and his head is tilted downward as if he is focusing intently on some aspect of the clay. Then, in the second, his left hand grips the table, fingers on the underside, thumb on the top, while the right hand holds the cutting tool just above the clay, and the man's tongue protrudes slightly from the right corner of his mouth. Then, in the third, the back of his left hand is pressed to his forehead, as if he is wiping sweat from his brow, while the right hand rests on the table, the palm pressed down on top of the cutting tool, and his jaw hangs slightly agape. And so on… The collective impression of these panels, if one strips away the detail, is hieroglyphic in nature, as if each unique position held represents a single character in some language[11a].

[11a] Which maybe is what is going on, or maybe this is something I have chosen, over time and reflection, to see in this, owing to something that Kellan had said to me during one of the few visits I was permitted in the year after Natalie's death. When I asked him what he was doing to keep himself busy, he told me he was working on a language that one could use to speak to the dead. His theory, apparently, was that our inability to communicate with the dead had to do not with the incompatibility of life and death but with the fact that we have no language for that sort of communication. At the time, I assumed this to be another of the impractical ideas that Kellan was prone to. His creativity was a wild phenomenon, producing a steady stream of designs, and when he ground them in this reality through his comics, they were brilliant, but they did not always make it to the page. Quite

often, the ideas would seek purchase in the material world and would just seem ludicrous (age ten: flying tree house, age fifteen: a color-coded clothing system for high school social hierarchy, age twenty-nine: portable lie-detectors for use in social situations). This "language of the dead" idea seemed like one of those. Had he written it into the hands of a character in one of his works, it would have been rich with meaning. But it seemed to me like his grief had him trying to rewrite the world, and it was hard to see this happening to him. It wasn't until three or so months after his disappearance that I even remembered this sequence of panels, at which point I began to wonder if what he was doing here was an attempt at the language he had postulated to me. I honestly don't know. I might be seeing more of him in this work than is actually there.

[12] Where I was originally thinking of the substance as mud, I began here to think of it as clay.

[13] And it becomes clear here, after some reflection (as in, I did not immediately understand this) that the face seen in the eye earlier was only in the eye figuratively. We were, in that moment, for how real it seemed, only seeing the inspiration for what the man is doing[13a].

[13a] Kellan no doubt did this on purpose. He wanted us to think we were seeing the face of the clay so that we would feel a particular concoction of unsettling emotions when we eventually discovered that the head was still faceless but for those lips. He said to me after Natalie's death that the hardest part for him was how, without her to attest to it with her presence, it was impossible to prove that she ever existed. I think he was trying to convey here the disorientation he felt because of this.

[14] Visible through use of the glasses, a galactic spiral made of what would be, if the clay head were made of flesh, hundreds or thousands of freckles.

[15] Natalie had no such birthmark on her face, but Kellan once told me something that might explain this: he said that when he looked into other people's eyes, which he did infrequently, it was like looking into a dark corner, but when he looked into Natalie's eyes, it was like looking through a window at the entire universe.

ISSUE 4

Cover: Same field, same moon. The pile of dirt is now higher. Only a half foot or so of the shovel handle is visible over the grassline.

Summary:

Opens on a woman's form, sculpted from clay, in a standing position next to the table from the previous issue. The image is presented from a modest angle so that even though the form is naked, nothing private is visible. A beam of light falls on the form through a ceiling-level basement window. Over the course of several panels, the view closes in on that beam, specifically on the particles of dust made visible by it[1]. Those particles move steadily in straight lines parallel to the direction of the beam. Suddenly, those particles swirl. They appear in one final panel arranged like a galaxy and then are sucked into a nose.

The man has entered the room. He is holding a clay shaping knife in one hand and a book in the other. He sits at the table, putting both the book and the knife down on top of it. He opens the book and turns the pages a few times. We then see two of the book's pages, presented in the comic as a two-page spread. The pages contain anatomical drawings of the female reproductive system, both the external and internal parts[2]. On the next page, the man, looking down into the book, speaks. "I don't think I can do this," he says. "I don't think I can give you one of these." The man stands up with the knife in his hand and walks to the side of the clay body. His eyes are level with the side of its head. "But," he says, "I want you to be… complete." The man walks to the other side of the clay body. He leans in close to the right side of its[3] face. He cuts a tiny piece of clay from its cheek. He holds that piece between his thumb and pointer finger, the way that one might hold an eyelash that has fallen off. He backs away, turns from the female form, holds the clay up to the light. His head drops. "I want *us* to be… whole," he says[4]. He leaves the room, but we do not. We remain in the room with the form for several panels[5].

The man returns to the room. He sits down again and studies the pages in the book. He stands up and approaches the clay form. He gets close but veers away at the last moment. He puts the knife in his mouth to free up his hands and rolls up his sleeves. He circles the clay form[6]. Once. Twice. Three times. He opens his mouth and lets the knife fall into his hands. He sits back down at the table and once again looks into the textbook. He reads quietly for several panels. Suddenly, he begins to read aloud from the text, a passage on the folds of flesh that frame the entrance to the female reproductive system[7,8]. He reads like this for the span of almost two pages of the issue, during which the center of the visual images in the panels slowly drifts from the man toward the clay form until, in the final panel of the sequence, only the clay form is visible and the recitation of the text bleeds into the panel from the unseen periphery[9].

The man stops reading and stands up from the table. He approaches the clay form again, looks at it, looks at the knife. He turns from the statue and throws the knife at the wall. The word "KLANG" is written in red ink across a panel in which the man is standing with his back to the back of the clay form, at a distance of several paces[10]. "What are we going to do?" he says. He turns to face the back of the clay form. "What are we going to do?" he says again. He waits several panels for an answer. "Forward no matter what?" he says. He reaches into his pocket and pulls out an ornate brass key. He presses the key through the clay of the back at the center of the torso until it has disappeared completely into the clay form. He repairs the surface where the key was inserted. Then he leaves the room a second time and returns with a small bucket that says "Chicken Fat" on it. He approaches the clay form. "This," he says, "has been sitting out in the moonlight for the past four hours." He puts the bucket down and scoops a handful of fat from it. He rubs the fat between his hands and begins to apply it to the clay form like sunscreen.

Notes

[1] The idea that Kellan had for a comic about a single photon (see Issue 2, note 2) was preceded years earlier by an idea (and also, if I remember correctly and am not making this up, some story panels) for a comic about a single particle of dust floating in a room. Though Kellan never said as much, I believe the dust idea evolved into the photon idea. He had the first just after the publication of the final issue of *The Harpoon Follies*, his reimagining of Melville's *Moby Dick*[1a]. He was at the peak of his success but feeling lost[1b]. I would find him at his apartment sitting mopishly at his desk, drawing weird, abstract patterns on index cards[1c]. Every so often, he'd fling the cards across the room and they'd amass on the floor like leaves (this period would eventually culminate in the creation of *The Mall Beasts*). The second idea came, as I've already said, well into his relationship with Natalie. I remember him doodling several panels on to a cocktail napkin at his wedding while waiting nervously at the bar for the public first dance that was Natalie's only "traditional" request of him for the occasion[1d].

[1a] Kellan has never read Melville's novel, so *The Harpoon Follies* are really more a reimagining of the zeitgeistial *Moby Dick* authored not by Melville but by the fame of the book itself.

[1b] It was just after his awful appearance on Australian television's *The Chevy O'Donnell Show*.

[1c] This drawing of patterns was something he'd been doing since grade school. He told me once that his mind was always drawing, and so my theory is that the patterns are what it produces whenever his imagination is overrun by melancholy. I think of them as images of his boredom.

[1d] She herself found most of the wedding "traditions" to be hollow but wanted this one dance because she could not dance with her father who had passed away several years earlier, right before she met Kellan.

[2] This is not the first time such an image has appeared in one of Kellan's works. A similar image can be found in *Cupcakes*, issue 4, where, in a flashback to his teenage years, Darby, the book's main character, tries to masturbate to images of female genitalia in a medical textbook he

has found, a desperate attempt, in the wake of an encounter with his mother, to "overcome" the desire that he feels toward other men. Kellan spent close to a month studying medical texts to develop the technical skills necessary to produce the two-page panel that was found at the middle of the issue[2a]. As a result of this, he acquired incidentally a highly specific knowledge of the female reproductive system, which he used to regale me with whenever he was too annoyed with me to express himself properly.

[2a] This panel is famous amongst his fans, some of whom, because Darby, immune to the sexual allure of it, experiences the vagina featured across the comic's centerfold like a Rorschach blot—he sees a series of different images in it, from a demon's face to a butterfly—have invented a Charades like game in which one teammate attempts to guess by way of silent clues what image the other teammate is seeing in the panel.

[3] I'm not sure if this is the correct pronoun to be using here. It's possible that it should be she. I have debated this for far longer than one would imagine. I've decided to use the neutral, but only because it feels the least uncomfortable.

[4] This entire sequence is highly melodramatic, breaking from the tone established over the previous three and a half issues[4a].

[4a] Kellan occasionally employs melodrama in his works when he wants to convey the insanity of life. His thought on this, expressed during a comic convention panel in response to Martha Villanova's criticism of *Crustacean Wedding* (whose three main characters, the ones forming the love triangle, she accused of being constantly engaged in a game of melodramatic footsie), is that nothing is truer to the madness of human culture and experience than how the worst of human writers unintentionally portrays the tensions of the human experience, and that those who cringe at these soap-operatic portrayals do so not because of how bad they are but because of how disgusting it is to see themselves so clearly[4b].

[4b] I think that here it was probably himself he wanted to be disgusted with, a twitch of the guilt he felt for having survived the accident.

[5] Though this issue began with just the clay form in the room, the reader (at least this reader), as the narrative returns to that state, is now suddenly aware of *being alone in the room* with the clay form (earlier the awareness, as it familiarized itself with the circumstances, was largely focused on the existence of the clay form and then taken in by the dust), and the mind of the reader (at least this reader) searches for something else to put itself into, a psychic escape pod through which to exit from the room and return to the body it calls home.

[6] He appears crazed as he does this, but Kellan gives us just enough of the expression on the man's face that we are aware of the discrepancy between his outward appearance and his interiority. We know that the man has not actually been reduced to the savage state indicated by how he circles the clay form with a knife in his mouth. We know even that he is unaware that he appears this way, that he is unaware that his actions are perceivable. He is, in this moment, a man divided at the intersection of body and mind, and we are being given the opportunity to witness what this quantitatively ephemeral incidence looks like.

[7] The word labia is never used. He reads seemingly from the middle of a passage, after the clinical term has been introduced.

[8] Because of its technical nature, I do not recall the exact text of the passage but presume that anyone interested in an approximation of what it contains could find such in the portion of any anatomy textbook that deals with the female reproductive system.

[9] I have had trouble deciphering what Kellan intended with this. I initially thought that he was trying to convey the loneliness of the man, particularly in the last image of the sequence, during which I felt, this time once again, alone in the room with the clay form, the man having been driven by his own loneliness deep into his head to some place of mild lunacy from whence he is spewing the words contained in the text almost autonomically (as for my own sense of loneliness in that moment, I wanted, I think, someone else to confirm for me that what the man was doing was universally unsettling, but the only other witness to this behavior was the clay form). But, after some consideration, I have found myself wondering if Kellan was trying to indicate that the man was, in lieu of reading to himself for some purpose of understanding, reading to the clay form for some purpose that only

he understood. Or if he was indicating that the clay form was somehow listening to the man, who *was* reading only to himself, (which interpretation makes the final panel all the more unnerving since suddenly it is no longer I who was seeking someone to commiserate with but the clay form seeking that commiseration from me). Or if Kellan intended all of this to dislodge the bearings of the reader; if perhaps this was some sort of swipe at the distance between fact and fiction[9a].

[9a] And the possibility also exists, as I think on this now, that Natalie's death had taken just such a swipe at that distance as it existed within Kellan, and here Kellan, having no other choice, is expressing that without any intention of pulling the reader into it. The reader is only pulled into it because the force of such a distortion is impossibly compelling.

[10] The image calls to mind a pistol duel.

ISSUE 5

Cover: Same field, same moon. The pile of dirt is now human height. The shovel is no longer visible.

Summary:

Close-up on the eyes of the clay face, which are closed. One full page panel of this. Two full page panels of this. Three full page panels of this. Another full page panel, but the eyes are open. On the next page, the entire clay woman is visible from above. She is lying in a bed on her back, in a yellow sundress, her arms at her side, her legs touching. She turns her head left without moving any other part of her body. She turns her head right. "Hello," she says to someone who is currently out of view.

The view shifts. The man is in the room, standing next to the bed. "Hello," he says. The woman sits up in the bed. "How long was I sleeping?" she says. "Not that long," says the man. "Did I miss anything?" says the clay woman. "Not really," says the man. "Are you hungry?" "I think so," says the clay woman. "I can make you something to eat," says the man. "How about breakfast?" "Breakfast sounds good," says the clay woman. "Eggs? Bacon?" says the man. "Yes, please," says the clay woman. The man leaves the room. The clay woman swings herself around to sit on the edge of the bed. She looks out a window and sees the sun. The view shifts: we see the clay woman's face, sunlight falling on her left eye and the part of her cheek that bears the galaxy mark.

The man is in the kitchen, cracking eggs into a steel frying pan. A close-up on a brown egg, the shell cracked at the bottom[1]. Further close-up on where the eggshell is broken. From that close perspective, the egg's internal matter slides from the shell slowly over several panels. The center of focus in these panels is the bright yellow yolk, on the surface of which parts of the kitchen are reflected. In one of these panels[2], the metallic handle of the frying pan can be seen on the yolk surface, and on the handle's surface (as it is reflected in the egg), a reflection of the man's face is visible[3]. He appears to be smiling[4]. Then, as we zoom back out to a more comprehensive view of the moment, we see the egg falling into the pan. From there, the man scrambles the eggs. When they are done, he places them on a plate next to three slices of bacon and a quarter cantaloupe[5].

The man enters the bedroom carrying a tray. He approaches the bed where the clay woman still sits on the edge looking out the window[6]. As he enters her periphery, she turns her head toward him. "Is all this for me?" says the clay woman. "Is it too much?" says the man. "No," says the woman. "It's perfect." The clay woman takes the tray from the man and places it on her lap. The man sits down next to her on the bed. The clay woman picks up a fork from the tray and begins to eat. "How is it?" says the man. "Delicious," says the clay woman. She picks up a piece of bacon with her hands and bites it in half. She eats the second half. She takes a few more bites of the eggs. Then she puts down the fork and turns her head to face the man, who has been trying not to watch her while she eats. "What is it?" he says. "I have a really good feeling about things," she says. "About what?" says the man. "Nothing," says the clay woman. "Everything. I don't know. Sometimes you're just alive, but sometimes you *feel* alive. This is one of those times, don't you think?" The view comes around to behind the man, centered on the back of his head, the clay woman's face, partially obscured, visible beyond it[7].

The view shifts back. The clay woman lifts the tray off her lap and puts it on the bed. "Let's go out back," she says. "To the backyard?" the man says. "Yes," says the clay woman. "Let's sit in the garden. It seems like a lovely day to sit outside and watch the sun coast through the sky." "I don't have a garden," says the man. "Then we can sit where you're going to have a garden," says the clay woman. She smiles. "Ok," says the man. The two stand up from the bed. As they leave the room, the view remains with the tray, closing in until what remains on it is clear: a single stick of bacon, a few curds of egg, and the cantaloupe. The view closes in so that only the cantaloupe is visible: it has not been touched at all[8].

Outside in the backyard, the man and the clay woman sit on the grass, their legs long before them. Their arms are slightly kicked back, propping their torsos up like tent poles. The view is from behind them, looking out toward the sky, the sun prominent in it. A sequence of panels in which the man and clay woman do not move, in which only the sun moves, arcing through the sky. "So," the man says finally. "So," says the clay woman.

Notes

---

[1] Kellan has captured the egg in this panel in the normally imperceptible moment when the shell has been busted open but the contents of the egg have yet to leak out. This might be foreshadowing, but it also might be Kellan's fascination with moments that exist unperceived or, more specifically, our inability to perceive those moments with our five senses even though we are able to deduce their existence intellectually. What interests him most about these moments is the possibility that we ourselves are made up of some, that our whole being consists not only of what we can perceive directly but also of certain elements that for whatever reasons we are unequipped to detect but which can be discovered deductively. In fact, he held, for quite some time, to a theory that we are made up entirely of such moments and that all of how we perceive ourselves is deductive, that perception itself is accomplished entirely through deduction, despite it seeming otherwise. He used to talk to me about this theory constantly, whether I wanted to hear about it or not. Then he met Natalie. He told me that she was his unperceivable self made visible, so in her, it was finally possible for him to see who he is. After that, he never mentioned the theory again.

[2] What I would call the main panel of this sequence.

[3] This was viewable only with the aid of the glasses and a great deal of attention. The image is complex. The face is pulled and distorted by the unusual shape of the handle, and to this distortion is added the distortion from the curvature of the yolk's surface and the impact of gravity upon that surface. It took me a while to reverse engineer the process so that the face made sense to me as a face.

[4] What strikes me most about this image is the great lengths Kellan seems to have gone to here to not only craft this smile but also to conceal it. It's almost as if he was determined to convolute the distance between the reader and the man's happiness.

[5] Cantaloupe was Natalie's favorite fruit and also her favorite breakfast.

[6] I found myself wondering here, since the reader is aware that enough time has passed for the man to prepare breakfast, upon what the clay woman has been transfixed for the duration. Is it something out the

window or in her head or even something inside the room with her reflected off the window glass? If it is in her head, is it an abstract thought, an image, a song, an entire world? If it is an entire world, what is that world like? Is it a world she has visited or a world that she is inventing? If it's a world she's inventing, how similar is it to the one she exists in? Could she, without knowing it, be imagining the world that Kellan and the reader are from? And so on. It is a small moment that grows exponentially as effort is put into dissecting it[6a].

[6a] Kellan always wanted to do a comic that consisted of only one such moment into which the reader would pour themselves to create an entire universe. He would pitch it every few years to his publisher and they would always decline.

[7] Given what happened earlier in the surface of the egg, I suspect that Kellan is using the man's head to obscure a smile on the man's face. I could be entirely reading into things, but it seems like a reasonable conjecture.

[8] Sometimes, it feels like Kellan is watching these events unfold even as they are created. I can almost sense him "behind the lens," staring at the cantaloupe, trying to understand how it remains uneaten, as if he had intended it to be eaten but it was somehow not eaten, as if the clay woman has a mind of her own, as if this universe is defined by rules that Kellan doesn't know about[8a].

[8a] Another way to put this is that this panel with the cantaloupe feels less like it is part of the man's story and more like it's part of Kellan's.

Cover: Same field, same moon. The pile of dirt, which has grown considerably in size, has assumed an amorphous but unnatural shape, reminiscent of a bemittened hand.

Summary:

The man sits at the dining room table. Across from him sits the clay woman. Between them: two candles burn. Before them: plates and food[1]. The man wears a gray suit with a white shirt and a pink and yellow striped tie. The clay woman wears a blue, off-the-shoulder dress. The man spears some food from his plate and takes a bite. "… and so," he says, "the store was out of lemons. Can you believe it? An entire supermarket, and not a single lemon. A thousand lemon flavored or shaped things, but not a single lemon. I wondered for a while if it might be possible to reclaim some of the lemon from a natural lemon-scented dish detergent, but I was skeptical that there's any actual lemon in lemon-scented products, even though it would explain where all the lemons went." He takes another bite of his food. "How does a supermarket run out of lemons? I told the manager, I said, 'hey guy, I had a dream last night about lemon pudding and now I want to make some, so how are you guys out of lemons?' He told me some story about a frost in Florida, and when I pointed to the mound of oranges he said the oranges were from California." The thin smoke coming off of one of the candles curls back into itself like an ocean wave starting to break. "And when I asked him how come California didn't send any lemons with those oranges, he asked me why the lemons were so important to me and I told him that I had a special dinner planned and that in the lemon pudding dream, my mother, who is still alive, came to me as a ghost and told me that in order to avoid misfortune I needed to serve the lemon pudding at the end of that dinner. Then he asked me if my mother had specified that the lemon pudding needed to be homemade and if not why couldn't I buy some pre-made lemon pudding which the store has in the refrigeration units of aisle four." He brings a glass of wine up off the table and toward his lips. "Isn't that a strange dream?" he says, the wine glass still unsipped from. "Have you ever dreamed of dreaming in a dream? I guess technically I didn't dream the dream with my mother in it. I only recalled it while I was talking to the supermarket manager." The smoke from the candle uncurls. "It's ok," the clay woman says, "I don't really like lemon pudding." The man laughs. "I know you don't like lemon pudding," he says, "but my mother was adamant." He laughs again. "Doesn't matter, though. There is no lemon pudding. How do you like the veal?[2]"

In the next panel, a giant red arrow hangs above the two, pointing to the center between them. In the panel after that one, the view zooms in to the microscopic space at the tip of the arrow (the arrow's tip is still visible in the upper right corner of this panel as a large red triangle). In this space, we see a pig with a halo and angel wings and a female mermaid with large, masculine muscles[3]. The pig holds a harmonica in one of its hands, the mermaid a cake. The two creatures[4] are facing one another. The angel-pig asks the mermaid for a slice of the cake. The mermaid turns away. The angel-pig offers to play the mermaid a song on the harmonica and, though the mermaid does not say yes, she does not say no. The angel-pig begins to play a song. Black musical notes flow out of the harmonica toward the mermaid[5]. As they near her, they coalesce into the "silhouette[6]" of a man and a woman. The music-note man bows respectfully before the music-note woman who coyly turns away from him. He races around to the other side of her and reaches into the pocket of a jacket he is wearing or else his chest[7] and pulls out a bouquet of flowers. The music-note woman scoffs. The man tosses away the flowers and reaches again into his jacket/chest, pulling out a pendant. Another scoff. Another toss. Another object produced: a valentine's heart-shaped box of candy or his heart, which looks like a comic rendering of a heart. The music-note woman scoffs once more. The music-note man swallows the heart / box of candy and reaches into himself a fourth time. This time he pulls out a bunny. The music-note woman giggles. He reaches into himself again and pulls out a knife. The music-note woman chuckles. He slits the bunny open and pulls out its skeleton. She laughs. He embraces her. They kiss.

The angel-pig stops playing the harmonica—the music notes and the scene they were creating disappear—and waits in silence for the mermaid's response. Finally, the mermaid pulls out a knife.

Before we are shown what she does with it[8], the perspective shifts back to the panel in which the man and the clay woman are sitting at the dinner table, the giant red arrow pointing to the exact center between them. Over the course of several panels, the red arrow retreats toward the upper right corner of the scene until it disappears completely. During these panels, the man and clay woman each take several bites of food from their plates. When the arrow is finally gone, the man puts down his fork and his knife. "Would you like to watch some tv?" he says.

Notes

[1] The food is amorphous, comic-strip style, little gray lumps. Kellan normally eschewed such conventions, but here he seems to be more interested in other things.

[2] Kellan can't cook. He has tried to learn but can never mix or balance flavors correctly. It bothers him endlessly, this inability of his, and as a result, the characters he creates are often good at or at least fixated on cooking. Natalie used to make fun of him for this [2a] (and get away with it; for years, I attempted to joke about this only to be met with sour looks or extended silences).

[2a] One time, for no particular reason, she threw Kellan a surprise party for which she enlisted the help of several chefs that she knew, whom she asked to produce real-world equivalents of the dishes that Kellan had invented through his characters. The menu for that evening included Chocolate and Cinnamon Pork Chops (*Clothespins and Circuses*), Shark and Tuna Stuffed Sunkissed Melon (*Brine Comedy*), Spicy Cheese Soup Dumplings (*D.ynamo, O. pera, S.ynergy*) and Peppermint Squid Ink Cupcakes (*Cupcakes*).

[3] Natalie had a mermaid tattoo on her left calf with standard mythological proportions. She used to joke that her younger self, the one who had gotten the tattoo, had been too naive and that had she, the older and more mature Natalie, been the one to get the tattoo, she would have made the frail looking mermaid hard and strong.

[4] It is my belief that these things are, in reality, supposed to be some sort of guardian spirits. In the scene that follows, we are witnessing a courtship exchange that occurs between these spirits.

[5] I have made a list of the three songs that I believe Kellan might have been imagining here. 1. "Angry Blister" by The Knock Knock Jam, a song that Kellan used to listen to on repeat for hours at a time 2. "Telegram" by Butter for the Bastard, to which he had his first slow dance with a girl in high school 3. "The Night is a Mandala" by Richter

Scam, a song that Natalie introduced him to that he made me listen to in my car.

[6] It's not a true silhouette, since the image is still made up of tiny musical notes and therefore contains spaces.

[7] The silhouette nature of the characters in this play within a play within a play makes it difficult to determine the specifics of this action, which is certainly intentional. Kellan has employed these tactics in a number of other places in his works, such as the fifteenth issue of *Crustacean Wedding,* an entire issue presented using only the characters' shadows in which each of the characters struggles with the others, in their own unique way, to keep the love triangle from imploding in the wake of one character's unfaithfulness to the group.

[8] The options here being, in my opinion, that she cuts the cake or cuts something else, the wings off the angel-pig perhaps.

ISSUE 6.5

Cover: Identical to previous cover except for an unexplained, pale white glow emerging over the horizon[1].

Summary:

The man and the golem[2] sit on a couch. The view is from directly behind them, the back of their heads and necks and shoulders visible above the couchline. Between their heads, a modern-looking flat screen television sits in the central rectangular space of an entertainment stand[3]. That space is framed by a series of square cubbies that form the outer edge of the portion of the stand that is not obstructed by the couch. Each of these nine perimeter cubbies contains a single object (in order clockwise from lowest left cubby, approx. 9 o'clock, to lowest right cubby, approx. 3 o'clock): a wooden unicorn[4], x[5], a large snow globe[6], a bottle of Sloppy Vega's ginger ale[7], y[8], a photograph[9], a magic eightball[10], a small analog clock[11], and z[12]. The cubbies' outside edges abut the edges of the panel, forming a frame around the upper three-fifths of the panel's content (this frame persists with almost no alteration in each of the panels in the issue, the exception being the hands of the clock, which move subtly as time passes). The viewpoint remains steady throughout the issue, the focus always on what is being broadcast between the two people through the television[13].

On the screen as the issue commences: a commercial, played out over the course of three panels, in which a bear and an anthropomorphized roll of toilet paper are roasting marshmallows over a campfire. No words are exchanged (though musical notes indicate the presence of some background, wordless jingle). The final panel, a yellow screen, proclaims, "Even bears know what's up." Then the programming returns to a television show that had been in progress. A man holds a knife to the throat of a woman. Across from them stands another man whose hands are held up and outward to demonstrate the absence of weapon or fist[14]. The open-handed man pleads with the other man to let the woman go. He says, "I understand." He says, "Sometimes, expressing your love for someone is like trying to describe a color." He says, "Sometimes, it gets violent." A close-up on the knife at the neck, followed by an even closer shot, followed by a trickle of blood from the woman's neck that hugs the knife before flowing gently downward, followed by a shot of the weaponless man's face, followed by a close-up on the left side of the face capturing the eye and the sideburn area, followed by the descent of a bead of sweat down the area between the eye and sideburn. "Try not to do that," the open-handed man says after the shot zooms outward, capturing the entire scene again. A painting on the wall behind everyone depicts a boat on a body of water[15]. The man with the knife barks like a dog at the other man. He sniffs the woman's neck. "Power," he says, "is not an exchange[16]. Maybe you don't understand the knife?"

The channel changes[17].

A man and a woman are running, hand in hand, through a corridor. The walls are dystopic technological constructs, like giant circuit boards. The two look distressed, their faces marked with terror and dirt, their clothing ripped and dirty. The wall behind them is covered in a shadow belonging to something off-screen, a shadow that is just humanoid enough to signal its belonging to something the viewer would project intelligence onto and also just creature enough, particularly the one visible appendage, a spear-like tail, to attribute to it a belligerence. The two humans rush around a corner. The man says, "Look, ahead. An exit." The woman says, "Don't you remember what the ship looks like from the outside? We have to be twenty feet up." The man says, "We'll have to jump." The woman says, "It's too high." The man says, "Land softly. Roll. Protect your knees. Don't ask too much of your bones." The man charges forward, pulling at the intersection point between himself and the woman. The woman gives in and begins her own charge. A severed human head passes them in the air as they run, presumably tossed by whatever is chasing them. The man looks down at the severed head as the two run by it, making prolonged eye contact with it as they pass. The woman says, "Is that…" The man says, "Not anymore." The woman says, "But…" The man says, "We are almost there. Don't stop at the edge. Jump. Protect your knees. Don't ask too much of your bones." The pair come to an open doorway. The man leaps out. As the woman crosses the doorway's threshold and begins her leap, a monstrous gray hand, gnarled and savage looking, grabs her hair, pulls her from the man's grasp and back into the ship. This action spins the man around so that he is no longer facing the ground as he falls but is instead looking up at the doorway he just exited through. Falling right behind him is one of the woman's shoes.

The channel changes.

A man and a woman sit behind a news desk. They have no faces[18]. The man says, "Victor plans to continue selling his meat-and-coffee cookies at the local flea market despite the protestors." There is a pause, a single panel in which the faceless people sit quietly at the desk[19]. Then the woman says, "In other news, RTS has obtained some disturbing footage from yesterday's earthquake in Rutnisia." New panel: she says, "A man and a woman were on their honeymoon, visiting Tsregatiu Canyon, the famous Rutnisian canyon, known more commonly as The Wishing Well. From what we understand, as the quake struck, the man was standing at the canyon's edge, tossing coins into the Sheigal river below for good luck, a common activity amongst tourists and locals alike. The woman was live streaming this from a few feet away. What you are about to see is difficult to watch." The image cuts in the next panel to a young man standing at the edge of a cliff, one of several people standing at the edge, but the only one interested in the camera lens. There is a headline banner at the bottom of the screen that reads "Death toll in Rutnisian Earthquake Approaches Five Thousand." The man says, "Just one more. This one for your mother. She asked me to. She gave me this specific coin." The man holds up the coin, but it is too far away to make out. From out of the shot, a woman says, "Why did she give it to you and not..." The rest of what is said is interrupted by an enormous cracking sound (the word CRACK is written in bold red letters diagonally across the part of the panel near where the woman's speech bubble is, obstructing the final words of her thought). The man is suddenly a foot lower in the shot. "Janie?" he says. The shot lunges toward the man, indicating that the woman, no longer concerned about the video but still holding the recording device reflexively, is taking action. The video angle, awkward and random, captures a hand reaching out to grab him. His hand reaches for the outstretched hand. The two hands come close to each at the center of the shot. Then one hand slips away. It slips farther away. It disappears. Here begins a complex sequence of images: presumably, the woman, in her shock, has dropped the recording device over the side of the cliff, and each panel is a single moment of the random footage being captured as the device falls through the air, nearly unintelligible glimpses of cliffside, of water, of an arm or leg that belongs to someone falling near the camera, of sky. The final image of the issue, visible between the heads of the two sitting on the couch in the living room—the one randomly captured moment that intersects with what a human operator would have wished to capture—is of the man, perfectly centered in the shot, falling, still reaching upward toward where the woman presumably stands at the cliff's new edge.

Notes

---

[1] Based on its quality as I recollect it, this glow was probably an allusion to the glow that is sometimes visible outside a home, coming through the window of someone watching television in the dark.

[2] After looking it up, I have decided that this is a better term than "clay woman."

[3] I don't know if this is the television with the cracked screen from the first issue, now repaired, or if it is a television bought to replace that television. It is only now, in retrospect, that I realize that both a broken television and a working television exist in this series.

[4] One of the robots in *A Conspiracy of Slumber* carries around with it a wooden unicorn identical to this. According to lore, it was that unicorn that first endeared Natalie to Kellan's work and consequently put her on the path to meeting him.

[5] Of the nine, I remember only six.

[6] Located in the upper left-most cubby of the stand. Using Mrs. Savoy's reading glasses, I was able to investigate the scene contained within the glass. It depicts a man and a woman in a row boat on a still body of water. With a little imagination, it is possible to conceive of them being cast down upon by the gentle falling of snow and to understand the awe of such a moment.

[7] A brand created originally in *Cupcakes* but appearing in many of Kellan's works, the soda of choice in the multiverse of his imagination. Kellan had a Sloppy Vega's bottle that a fan of his had sent him as a gift, which sat on a shelf in his bedroom until Natalie, angry at Kellan for his cold, logical reluctance to move in with her, tripped over a shoe that Kellan had left near the bed and into the shelving unit, knocking the bottle to the ground where it broke, spilling what Kellan described to me as a fabulous yellow liquid that emitted a foul, gingery odor. The smell drove him to live at Natalie's place for close to month, precipitating the eventual sale of Kellan's condo and permanent cohabitation.

[8] Of the nine, I remember only six.

⁹ Inspection using the glasses revealed the photograph to be a stock image that Kellan copied from an actual frame I saw in Kellan's apartment during one of the few visits I made to him while he was working on *Window Eyes* (the image is of a man holding a boy who is supposed to be his son). The frame had been purchased prior to the accident and had been slated to hold an image from some future event in Kellan and Natalie's life[9a]

[9a] The purchasing of a photo frame with the intention of filling it with a photo from an experience that had not yet materialized was something they did each year, a tradition carried over from Natalie's pre-Kellan life, established by Natalie to inspire against life's tendency to lethargize if left unchecked.

¹⁰ Located in the upper right-most cubby of the stand, creating an oppositional symmetry with the snow globe, to which it is identical in size.

¹¹ I know from some of the images that Kellan gave me long ago that he associated death with clocks. I suppose that this is something that any serious fan of his would know too from the scene in *D.ynamo O.pera S.ynergy* in which the dead of Farce are seen turning a wheel beneath the country's main citadel, a wheel that purportedly generates the passage of time in the universe.

¹² Of the nine, I remember only six.

¹³ Everything that takes place on the television was viewed using the glasses.

¹⁴ The faces of the woman and the weaponless man are not blurry, but their features are somehow nondescriptive. I think the best way I can convey this effect is to say that while these two have recognizably ordinary human faces, it is impossible to describe these faces to another person. Any description would simply suggest a face undistinguished from all other faces, a no doubt carefully plotted artistic maneuver by my friend[14a].

[14a] Something new for him, which, knowing him as I do, I'm sure he had been working on for a number of years up to its deployment here, probably for some other project that he had been planning prior to the accident.

[15] Had this been anyone else's work, I wouldn't have noticed details such as this, but it was these sorts of details that Kellan spoke to me about more than anything when we talked about his works-in-progress. Yes, he would talk to me about the larger things he was trying to accomplish, but he always seemed so focused on the little touches. For instance, he once called me four times over the course of a weekend to talk about what type of sports ball he should place in the corner of a garage in *The Mall Beasts* (those familiar with that work might know that he chose a tennis ball). These touches seemed to mean a lot to him. I think he felt that there was a limited degree of sincerity available in large gestures, that their size somehow warped reality artificially, or that at some point, the size of the gesture called so much attention to itself that its sincerity was necessarily tampered with, and while he accepted this as an unavoidable consequence of art, he also felt it necessary to compensate with smaller gestures, things that one was not supposed to notice but that when noticed would transmit something personal and pure between the creator and the one who noticed it, something free of artifice, like a doodle found in the margins of a notebook a student uses to take notes in math class[15a].

[15a] On a personal level, it saddens me that I am unable to remember many of these details available in *Window Eyes* and therefore can't provide the reader an experience true to who my friend is.

[16] This feels similar to something said by Maryanne in issue six of *Maze on Dixon*, in which she and Seraphim stage a reenactment of Superland's civil war using coffee cups and sugar packets. "Power," she says at one point, "is never having to say yes to someone."

[17] Kellan drew a panel that captures the almost imperceptible instant between channels, during which the television screen in the room is projecting a senseless reproduction of the absence of content, what looks like a poorly defined white stripe running across the middle of the screen. He borrowed this effect from much older televisions, the ones that hurled particles through a vacuum at the back of the screen (modern televisions operate much differently)[17a].

[17a] This panel reminds me of the phase Kellan went through in college where he was fascinated with those older televisions. He attempted an art project for one of his art classes that involved filling the vacuum tube

of a television with some sort of refractive medium without impeding the television's operation. He destroyed three televisions before finally giving up on a task that was far outside his expertise. Eventually, he would "successfully" "reproduce" this experiment in *The Mall Beasts,* Issue 5, in which Mandela, the bohemian yoga instructor invited to live in the secret tunnel settlement that the mall's janitorial staff has built for themselves and their families beneath the mall, fills several televisions with different substances–water, melted butter, maple syrup, urine–and in each we get a glimpse of what Kellan imagines the substances would do to the famous appearance-of-color scene from *The Wizard of Oz.* In the water, we see the world of Oz on fire, in the butter we see Dorothy standing on the Las Vegas Strip at the entranceway to a casino, in the syrup we see her masturbating one of the flying monkeys, and in the urine we see a family sitting at a dinner table, the matriarch passing the salt to the patriarch past their three dull-eyed offspring.

[18] Kellan hated the news in all its forms. He saw it as a vile marketing mechanism, disguised as an intellectual resource, pushing anti-individuality, anti-creative agendas. All news personnel in his works are portrayed without faces and are often employed by totalitarian forces[18a].

[18a]An example of this are the Coglodites in *Ratio of Sanity,* the blank-white-mask-wearing mouth pieces of the Cog, the ruling body of Escovailia that Otello is expunged from.

[19] In every instance in which Kellan has employed these faceless newsies throughout his career, there is always a panel like this one in which the faceless sit silently. The effect is always uncanny, for myself and others that I have spoken to about this: we all remember seeing faces where there aren't any.

ISSUE 7

Cover: Same field, same moon. The pile of dirt has now assumed a distinctly humanoid but otherwise featureless shape.

Summary:

The issue begins with a walk shown through a lengthy montage of scenes featuring the man and the golem dressed in casual clothing—jeans and a t-shirt for the man, a warm weather, sleeveless short dress for the golem. They are located in the center of each panel in this sequence (there are two equal size panels on each page, situated one above the other), front facing, side-by-side, holding hands. Their free limbs are adjusted slightly from one panel to the next, capturing them in different moments of their strides, capturing also other actions tangential to the walking such as pointing to objects both inside the panel with them and objects outside the view. The setting around them changes dramatically from panel to panel, eschewing continuity of the walk in favor of breadth of traverse. They appear in a park, on a street in a Chinatown, leaving a movie theater[1], entering a restaurant, at a mall, at a carnival, on a street in the Ethiopian section of town (flanked on both sides by an oversaturation of Ethiopian restaurants)[2], in a museum, on a beach, on a pier, in a large flower garden, in a vendor aisle of what appears to be a dental convention, inside a subway car, at the bottom of an escalator having just disembarked, in a dark alley[3], passing a water park[4], in a 1980's style video game arcade, in a pet store, passing the window of a jewelry store[5], moving away from a sunrise… and other places[6]. Sometimes, people in the background stare or gesture disconcertingly at them. Their clothing also changes (though it is always the same arrangement: jeans and t-shirt, sleeveless dress), as does the color of the leaves in the trees that are visible in some of the scenes (indicating that at least several weeks, if not months, are passing from the beginning of the montage to its end), and, most importantly, their facial expressions[7]. The changes to their faces are subtle and occur in a way that is difficult for the reader to comprehend. Are they growing heavier and more weary? Are they growing sleepy? Disconnected? Or merely pensive? For certain, there is a tension building through this change in the expressions, but that too is hard to understand. Is it love? Is it that strange space that forms between people as they fall in love with each other, that fear of admission, of rejection? Or is it some minor hostility building toward animosity? Is it an anxiety?[8]

Then, the last few pages of the issue: a return to the house, sudden and abrupt[9], to the bedroom specifically or the space where the bedroom and hallway meet. The man stands in the hallway, just beyond the bedroom's doorway. The golem is in the bedroom, lying on the bed. The scene is divided by the bedroom wall (the architectural insides of which are visible to us). The wall is presented at a slight angle so that we are able to see the plane of the doorway on the man's side of it. The golem calls out to the man. "Come," she says. But the man doesn't move. He drops his head and looks away from the golem. "Do you ever miss yourself?" he says. "I don't mean your right now self. I'm talking about missing who you used to be." The golem doesn't answer the question. "Come," she says again. But the man still doesn't move. "I've been thinking about this a lot lately," he says. "I miss who I was as a child and also as a teenager and who I was when I was twenty-four. I don't mean that I wish I was still those versions of me. I mean that who I am now would love to spend time with them, to see them again, to just be able to be together with them. Time is so frustrating. Why can't we co-exist with who we were?" The golem gets off the bed and begins to cross the room toward the man. "I want you," she says. The man keeps his head down. "I just don't think that it's necessary for everything to be so linear," he says. "Or if everything has to be so linear, why do we long in such a nonlinear fashion? Why are our emotions so fractal?" The golem closes in on the doorway. "Take me," she says. The man's head rises. He looks through the portal at the golem. "We can't," he says. "You aren't made that way." The golem is undeterred. She reaches through the doorway and begins to slide her arms around the man (the wall continues to divide and obscure parts of this). "No," the man says. But she continues to come. As her lips approach within inches of his, he pushes her away, not violently, but assertively. The golem steps back a few feet, comes to a stop, and is visibly confused. She remains like that for a few panels[10]. The grandfather clock is visible behind her in the background. Suddenly, the clock chimes the hour. The golem, as if in response to this, crumbles into dust.

Notes

---

[1] According to the marquee, there are three movies showing: *Punching Bag*, *Cupcakes* and *Mytosis*[1a]. On the left side of the entranceway is a poster for *Mytosis*, featuring Quaalude, the series's antagonist, standing in front of a mirror, looking to the left of his reflection while an unreflected version of himself stands next to him on the left.

[1a] Kellan is staunchly opposed to translating his comic books into movies or television shows, feeling as he does that the real beauty of the comic medium comes from how the focus is placed on a single moment at a time, and that where the motion in films and TV is a motion through time and space, the motion in the still frames of a comic book have to take place across a different set of axes, such as range of emotional invocation and depth of contemplation, axes that Kellan believes are more real than time and space. I don't 100% know why he suddenly imagines his comics as movies. My best guess is that this is a joke of sorts, one that Natalie would have found humorous?

[2] Ethiopian was Natalie's favorite food, which was a problem for Kellan who hated having his hands dirtied (he was not so terrible as to need the constant protection of gloves but balked at touching anything that could leave behind a moist residue). When they would go to Ethiopian restaurants, Kellan would jury-rig a claw with two forks, a rubber band and a napkin (something he learned from his few excursions to Japanese restaurants, where the waitstaff would make him what I always liked to call "beginner's chopsticks," chopsticks that are bound by a rubber band around a hinge joint–usually a rolled up napkin–so they can be used with a simple pinching motion that is regulated by the rubber band's tension). He would use this device to drop a piece of injera on to a pile of food and then scoop up the injera with some of the food tucked into it. It was absurd, but Kellan felt that if he had to go, he would attempt to have what seemed to him to be the correct experience. And not going wasn't an option. Natalie made it clear from the start what things she would abdicate to Kellan's peculiarities, and Kellan, over time, acclimated himself to the sacrifices that were necessary, a process in which he sometimes involved his works as a sublimating medium for

the rage and frustration and sorrow these sacrifices produced, an example being the violently depicted deadly food fight that Lushly quasi-accidentally provokes between the militaries of Farce and Province in *D.O.S.*

[3] Kellan had a strange fascination with dark alleyways, often choosing to walk through them when other, better-lit, safer, and even quicker routes were available. I think that, in general, he had a strange relationship to fear, oftentimes excessively fearful of things that most people didn't consider to be fear-worthy (like getting food on his hands) but also unafraid of what most people would consider to be frightening situations.

[4] Another inside joke. Kellan, as would be easy to surmise, hated waterparks, thought obsessively of the microscopic filth that inhabited the park's essential medium; and of course, Natalie, because of fond memories she had of yearly visits to a waterpark with her father, adored them and, knowing of Kellan's disdain, would, when she was frustrated with him for some minor reason, threaten to leave him and go live at one.

[5] Though clearly (almost too clearly) not the jewelry store that Kellan paced in front of for hours each day for nearly two weeks while he worked up the courage to buy Natalie an engagement ring, not for fear of commitment, as would be the case with many men, but for fear of the traditional, of being pulled into the black hole of convenience and stagnation that he associated with the status quo (see *Ratio of Sanity*, Issue 5, in which Otello struggles to free himself from a visual depiction of this phenomenon); a battle really between that fear and the love he felt for her.

[6] that I do not remember well enough to put in print.

[7] Or second-most importantly? Little bits of the golem seem to flake off as the panels move deeper into the progression. It took me a while to come to this interpretation of the little specks that occurred in the golem's aura[7a]. They were subtle enough to seem like incidental pencil marks but appeared with just enough regularity to make their being accidental improbable. I thought they might have been small bugs or a feeling of some kind represented abstractly, but in the end, flakes made the most sense.

[7a] It seems to me that Kellan went to great lengths to present the flaking as something to be discovered/understood upon reflection and not as a direct part of the initial reading experience, which is why I have decided to put this information in the notes and not the main text.

[8] I recognize that it is odd to present speculation as description, but it has proven impossible to capture the specific, highly contoured nebulosity of what Kellan has done here in any other way.

[9] Kellan's narrative style has always been abrupt and rough. He has never been particularly concerned with aesthetic fluidity, preferring instead work that, in its coarseness, calls attention to the inviolable seamlessness of our world, the way in which everything in the world, no matter how broken our personal sense of right and wrong and perfection might cause the world as a whole to appear, constantly orbits into and out of every other thing. But this work in particular exhibits a higher-than-normal degree of roughness, almost as if it is constantly engaged in an argument with comfort and propriety.

[10] We are, in ways that I am unable to explain, invited to come into these panels with her, to stop in these panels and experience her confusion.

ISSUE 8

Cover: Same field, same moon. The humanoid-shaped pile of dirt has now assumed the form of a woman.

Summary:

The man sits at the dining room table. Across from him sits a golem. Between them: a bowl full of lemons. Before them: plates and food[1]. The man wears a blue, button-down, long-sleeve shirt and a pair of khaki pants. The golem wears a blue, off-the-shoulder dress, a galaxy mark visible on her cheek. For several panels, they fork little gray lumps from their plates to their mouths. Then the man speaks: "Aren't these lemons great?" he says[2]. "They're from three different stores. I went to five stores today looking for only the best lemons. Two of the stores had only aging lemons and so I didn't buy any, but in the other three stores, I found lemons in an assortment of conditions, and after sifting through them, was able to find these. I'm not going to call them perfect. I'll call them vibrant. I found the most vibrant lemons possible, just like my mother asked me to." The golem looks up from her plate. "Your mother asked you to?" she says. "Not my *mother* mother," the man says. "My mother was in the dream I had last night. Didn't I tell you about the dream?" "Not that I remember," says the golem. "But I think that sometimes I forget things that I feel like I would remember, like other people's dreams. When I try to remember the dreams that people have told me about, I can't. Maybe you told me about it, and I forgot." "Well," says the man, "my mother came to me as I wandered a vast desert and handed me a shopping list that had only one item on it: the most vibrant lemons possible. I said to her, 'Mom, I've been wandering this desert for months. There are no lemons here. I love you, but I can't do this.' And you know what she said back?" In the next panel, where what the man is saying would be concluded, there is a speech bubble, but it is empty. The effect is that the man and golem appear trapped in a moment that spins forever without purpose. The look on the golem's face, the look of someone listening to something that is never going to be said, conveys an unsettling sense of fathomless expectation[3].

On the next page, the pair are walking again as they did in the previous issue. This sequence happens more rapidly than it did before, which is to say that it takes place across two six-panel pages (the panels are consequently smaller than the half-page panels of Issue 7). Most of the locations are ones from earlier: a park, Chinatown, a movie theater, a mall, a museum, a beach, a subway car, the bottom of an escalator having just disembarked, a dark alley… Their attire here is wintery (hats, scarves, etc.) and the trees no longer have leaves[4]. As the sequence unfolds, the expressions on their faces follow a progression similar to the progression exhibited by the man and the original golem, but because it happens more rapidly, it possesses an increased urgency[5], a franticness[6], a desperation.

Another abrupt transition: a return to the house, to the couch where in Issue 6.5 the man and the original golem watched television together. The view this time, at the outset, is from in front of them (neither the television nor the shelving system that contains it are visible). The man and golem sit toward the couch's center, a foot apart. In front of them is a small coffee table. Between them, resting on the palm of the golem's left hand (her central hand in this arrangement) is an open, coffee-table-book sized book. The two are looking down into the book's pages. "This is one of my favorites," the golem says. The framing shifts and we see the book from their perspective. The pages contain four black and white photographs of a woman lying in a bed. She is, in all the photos, curled up beneath a blanket, the right side of her head resting on a pillow, oblivious to the photo being taken above her. Her eyes, both of which are visible from the angle of the photo, are empty in that way of despair, like they, instead of being a causeway, as they usually are, are plugging up the channel between self and world. The page turns. More photos of the same woman lying in bed. Her position shifts from one picture to the next and the clothes that she is wearing changes, but in each, the eyes are the same[7]. The page turns again. And again. The same woman is on every page that the man and the golem look at[8]; the constant in her extremely limited but still shifting world: her eyes[9]. The scene shifts back to the couple on the couch, the same view from the front. Both of them are still looking into the book. "Isn't she beautiful?" says the golem. "Isn't she the most beautiful woman in the world? I don't love her because of the pain she feels. I love her because I think she feels it so that we don't have to." The golem looks up at the man, but the man continues to look into the book. His expression suggests he is struggling to understand something. "Do you find her attractive?" says the golem. "What?" says the man without looking up. In the next panel, before the golem responds, the man looks at her. The panel after that, "Do you find her attractive?" the golem says. "I don't know how to answer that," the man says. She puts the book down on the table in front of them. She leans toward the man. "What about me?" she says. The man looks away, toward the book on the table. The golem approaches his right ear and nibbles on the lobe. The man turns his head away. "We can't," he says. "You still aren't made that way." The golem sits back. For the next three panels, she stares at the man. During these panels, the man's head turns ever so slightly in her direction until in the last of them, he can see her out of the corner of his eyes. Then his head turns away and his eyes dart upward, looking toward the ceiling or some part of the house beyond the ceiling, like he has heard something. In the panel after that, the golem crumbles into dust.

The man slumps on the couch, his head no longer turned in any direction. He remains there next to the pile of dirt for two or three panels. Then he gets up from the couch and disappears from the scene, leaving the reader alone with the pile. He returns a few panels later with a broom and a bucket. Carefully, he sweeps the dirt off the couch and into the bucket. He carries the bucket through the study[10] and into the backyard.

We see him with a shovel. He digs for several panels and then pours the dirt from the bucket into the hole he has dug. He fills the hole in with some of the dirt he removed from the earth in the digging. He bends over, picks up a stick and places it into the ground to mark the location of the hole. He stands up and walks away. The scene zooms out and we see that there are two other upright sticks in a row with the one he just planted.

Notes

---

[1] The food is once again amorphous, a true departure from the detail with which he rendered the many dishes found in his work, particularly *Brine Comedy.*

[2] At this point, I imagine that the reader is beginning to wonder why there is so much talk about lemons. To be honest, I did not notice it at the time of my reading[2a]. It was only once I was recollecting for the purpose of this manuscript that the lemons stood out to me (strange how something so obvious could have remained elusive for so long). Off the top of my head, I have no knowledge of a relationship between Kellan and lemons. He has never spoken of them more than anyone else would, has never told me any stories about Natalie that involved lemons, has, as far as I know, never used them even incidentally in another of his works (and I know as far as having gone back through everything in search of a reference to them, including the pages Kellan gave me when we were children). I can offer only this possibility: After a few weeks of thinking about this, I called Sharon Savoy (who I have tried to disturb as little as possible) and asked her if there was any significance that lemons held for Kellan. She told me at the time that she couldn't think of anything but called back a few days later to tell me that she'd remembered something from Kellan's childhood. Apparently, when he was six, he went through a phase where he was fascinated, from an artistic perspective, with human organs[2b]. He practiced drawing them every day for months, and though he became quite good at drawing almost all of them, he never mastered the human heart. He drew hundreds of them and every single one of them had the same flaw: they were all too lemon shaped.

[2a] I didn't notice so many things, given the late hour and time constraints, and sometimes I wonder what details I missed, small or large, and even what significant things I've forgotten or remembered inaccurately or possibly even invented; sometimes I regret that you must experience this work through the sorry lens of myself.

[2b] She couldn't recall how this fascination had developed but thinks it might have been after seeing an anatomical drawing in a doctor's office.

[3] In fact, the golem, in my opinion, looks diseased, like she has been stricken with a strange illness.

[4] The golem seems to flake in these panels just as in the similar panels from the previous issue (see Issue 7, note 7).

[5] And because I knew at this point what happened last time, the tension/anxiety of the prior walk appeared here to me as despair.

[6] It feels to me almost as if Kellan himself found it difficult to relive the creation of these panels and so moved through them at an accelerated pace. I did not think to examine the panels more closely at the time, but I suspect that the level of detail in them would be comparatively diminished, the exception being the flaking, which was certainly more pronounced[6a], either by intention or because everything else has been lessened.

[6a] It was still subdued, but I knew at this point to look for it.

[7] Natalie suffered from bouts of severe depression, the longest of which lasted close to three months. She would remain in bed for the duration, quiet and crushed, not even crying (she, who was open about these episodes with people she trusted, told me once that the pain was otherworldly, in relation to which crying seemed useless). She needed others, either Kellan or her mother, to make her eat and drink (in that way alone was she a danger to herself). During these episodes, Kellan would be frantic. After the first few, he told me that it was his inability to comprehend the despair, the impossible irrationality of it, that drove him crazy. It made no attempts to justify itself and was irresponsive to logic. It seemed to exist purely because it existed and was therefore immune to solution. During the last of these episodes, though, he amended his original assertion and said that what truly broke him was how irrational *his* response to it was, how, no matter how bottomless her despair was, he always found enough love to meet it. As he lay beside her day after day, holding whatever small parts of her the despair left behind in the world while it enveloped her spirit, he faced the endless nature of the love he possessed, was forced to see that the love was beyond all qualification and therefore rationally annihilating. And so, it is not as strange as it might seem that Kellan would, in a way, commemorate these episodes. They were a significant part of the life that he and Natalie shared, and in the aftermath of that life, where we

might anticipate him having the desire to make it perfect, he is engaged by the desire to make it whole again.

[8] Whether because this woman is the sole focus of the entire book or because the golem is focused on the section of the book that contains photos of this woman, I can't say.

[9] To be clear, the woman is not Natalie, though I suspect that what we find in her eyes is what Kellan saw in Natalie's during Natalie's episodes.

[10] We see no other rooms in the interim, and though it is possible that the study is adjacent to the room with the television, the layout of the house remains elusive.

ISSUE 0[1]

Cover: The man sits at a table, eating mud from a soup bowl.

Summary:

The basement room once more. Another golem, placed on what looks like a homemade gynecological examination table. The angle of view is from the side. Its legs are in the stirrups, lifted and spread apart[2]. The man is sitting in a chair, positioned between the legs. A bucket on the floor next to his foreground leg. While neither his hands nor the area of the golem they work on are visible, it can be inferred that he is carving something into the clay where the legs meet the torso. From panel to panel, for about a page or so, his arms move. Finally, he sits up and his hands fall away from the golem's body. A pause. Then, a wail of frustration (an "arghhhhhh"). The man violently digs his hands into the clay he has just been working and scoops out what he has done. He tosses what he has scooped across the room. It lands on the floor, next to other mounds of clay. In the centerfold of the issue, a blowup of these mounds reveals that each of them is a rendering of female genitalia, created with vivid, life-like details[3,4,5].

The view returns to him. He is retrieving more clay from the bucket and packing it into the golem's pelvic region. When he is done, he retrieves the tools he was using previously from the ground and returns to work on the next attempt. He starts to whistle or hum: little music notes in a speech bubble. Over the next panels, the view gradually closes in on the speech bubble itself, gradually cuts the man and the golem out of the scene until, in the final panel of the issue, there is just white space with a single musical note at the center[6,7].

Notes

---

[1] This issue, though numbered 0, was, in the bundle of issues that Kellan presented to me (a bundle that was tied together with twine), found between issues 8 and 9 and depicts an event that seems to occur in the series's timeline between those issues. It is not a full-length issue, having what I remember as being only a handful of pages that had I not known Kellan as well as I do, I would have assumed were thrown together as an afterthought or else were mock-ups for what would eventually be a full-length issue.

[2] The golem does not move during the issue, and so I have assumed that it has not yet been brought to life.

[3] Each of them is hyper-realistic. In the context of the more traditional comic book style that Kellan has been employing throughout the work–which generally aims for a far more fantastical realism, one that is softer on the eye than unartificed reality–this makes them extra grotesque. Kellan, though it was uncommon for him, has employed such a contrast before, the two most well-known examples being his portrayal of *Static If*'s The Bruise, a hemophiliac vigilante who has the compulsive habit of eating his own blood-soaked bandages, and *Windmill Betty*'s Henrietta Periwinkle, a bulimic painter who would binge and then purge onto a canvas.

[4] Whatever it is that has displeased the man about these iterations remains a mystery.

[5] It is possible that the entire process here is an on-the-nose reference to Kellan's struggle to remember how Natalie had been built. I know him ell enough to know the kinds of things he might obsess about, and the realization, in the wake of her departure, that he had never paid close enough attention to this one prominent detail about her could certainly have been one of them. I can easily imagine him contemplating all the forces that had worked to make her invisible to him in that way, the shames and the inhibitions, and each of them would have seemed to him to speak to weaknesses in his love for her. Of course, the question then arises: Is what we see carved into the clay here his failed attempts at conjuring what had belonged to Natalie? I can't say for sure, but I

think yes, probably. While that might seem like a coarse or selfish thing for him to do, Natalie was someone unashamed of her body (like no small minority of artists, she had spent time just after art school working as a nude model for art classes) and would not have seen what Kellan did as a violation of her privacy but as a celebration of her totality. Which, I think, would have contributed to Kellan's obsessing since he likely would have felt that had the situation been reversed, Natalie would have remembered him with great clarity; and then at the core of this, of course the desire that the situation *had* been reversed, stressing and stressing and stressing him, alive in this work as one of the carefully contained subtexts competing for attention: what appears to be a widower tormented by his inability to remember what his wife's vagina had looked like is in fact that widower expressing guilt that he had survived what his wife could not.

[6] And so here too, this sudden music, another expression of Kellan's guilt about surviving?

[7] This issue contains a number of blank pages at the end. Kellan obviously wanted the close-in on the failures to be the centerfold, but the issue was complete before the right side of the parchment sheets were used in their entirety.

ISSUE 9[1]

Cover: The moon is visible in the sky from what appears to be the bottom of the hole. Shadowy blades of grass hang over the hole's edge.

Summary:

The man sits at the dining room table. Across from him sits a golem. Between them: a jar of lemon juice. Before them: plates and food[2]. The man wears a pair of white underwear briefs and a white tank top. The golem wears a blue, off-the-shoulder dress and has a galaxy mark on her cheek. They eat quietly for several panels. The man's shoulders are slumped. He is looking at his plate. In these panels, the man is also surrounded by faint squirrely lines[3], an aura of some kind that is ruffled or agitated[4]. Then the golem speaks: "I was thinking today about the word 'apart.' If you say that you feel apart of things, it indicates alienation. But, if you say that you feel a part of things, it indicates inclusion[5]. Isn't that strange? The space between the words somehow brings things closer." The man does not look up from his plate. He continues to eat as she is speaking. "Is there a word for that?" she continues (there's a panel between when she concludes this statement and speaks again in which both are silent), "Is there a word for when language betrays itself? Is it just irony? It feels like more than irony." Again, the man continues to eat (again a silent panel between the golem's statements). "We should invent a word for that," she says. "But what if someday that word becomes victim to or party of a betrayal?" (Another silent panel) "I suppose that's the risk whenever you create something. Why is that? Do all things suffer the potential to betray themselves or is it only things that people create? Is it a part of nature or a flaw in us?" The man looks up from his plate, but not at the golem. He looks at the bottle of lemon juice. He reaches for the bottle, opens it and drinks from it. He puts it back down, returns to his food. A final silent panel at the bottom right of a right-hand page.

Following that panel, there is a two-page advertisement for The Munduson Company targeting comic book readers, enthusiastically informing them of the wide variety of comic book-related paraphernalia—t-shirts and beach towels and pajamas and limited edition cereals—that are carried worldwide in their stores. The ad is unsophisticated as far as ads go. It is essentially a black background with bright yellow lettering, featuring, across the centerfold, Moosipher Munduson, Munduson's anthropomorphized moose mascot[6], wearing a t-shirt that says, "To be nice is every superhero's greatest challenge."[7]

On the next page, a walk sequence. The page contains twenty-four panels. The attire here is nonsensical: the man is wearing shorts and flipflops with a heavy winter jacket, the golem is in a ball gown. The trees, when there are some, no longer have leaves on them, but it is not the barrenness of winter depicted: the trees look scorched or burned out. Some of the panels visit many of the places from the first two walks: a park, Chinatown, a museum, a beach, the bottom of an escalator having just disembarked, a dark alley… The other panels feature the man and golem walking through white (parchment colored) space. As the sequence unfolds, the expressions on the man's face remain blank. The golem's face follows a progression similar to the previous progressions.

Once more, an abrupt return to the house, this time to the study. The man, alone, wearing a suit, looks through the drawers of the desk. The golem calls to him from the other room. "Come," she says. "I'm waiting." He closes a drawer he is looking in and crosses the room. The backyard is visible through the windows in the background as he crosses. Dozens of sticks have been planted in the ground[8].

The man appears at the bedroom door. The view is from behind him. Over his shoulder, the golem is partially visible on the bed, lying on her side, her head propped up on her hand (the hand supported by the elbow's contact with the mattress), her left leg stacked on her right, the area between her collar bones and her knees obscured by the man's body in the doorway. There's no clothing on her shoulders and none on her knees (or below them), and so it is to be assumed that she is naked. In the next panel, the golem says something, but the speech bubble that contains the words is partially obscured by the man's head just as her body is partially obscured by his body; only the curved edge of the bubble and a few tiny fragments of letters (too truncated to be identified) can be seen[9]. Then, a panel identical to the preceding one, minus the speech bubble, indicating the man's silence in response to whatever the golem said. And then another panel with a blocked speech bubble (the little bits of letter visible at the edges of what is being said are distinctly different, indicating different letters, indicating different words being hidden). And then another indicating silence. This cycle repeats for two pages, the panels changing only slightly: in addition to the letter fragments (which exhibit distinct deviations from previous iterations), the man's posture shifts subtly as he stands in the doorway, the golem's head and legs shift subtly as she lies on the bed, his posture shifting more frequently than her head and legs, indicating a restless excitement or discomfort within him[10].

The man finally moves toward the golem[11]; the view remains behind the man from some point outside the room, and over the course of several panels, he grows smaller relative to the doorway. The view shifts to capture the man climbing on to the bed with the golem. He remains fully clothed, the presumption that the golem is naked is now established as fact, though only a single exposed breast is visible. The man falls on to his side, mirroring the golem's position. The golem reaches out with her left arm and puts her hand on the center of the man's chest.

The scene cuts to an image of a human heart[12] being pounded on from two angles by small sledgehammers.

The scene cuts back to the bed. The golem is lying flat on her back. The man hovers over her, his head bent toward hers. They are kissing. The man pulls back. "Are you ok?" he says. "Am I too heavy?" "No," she says, "not too heavy at all." They resume kissing. The man's clothing crumbles off of him. They continue to kiss. As this happens, the man's face begins to disappear into the golem's face. The perspective closes in on this happening to highlight the two significant elements of it: the distortion of the man's face as parts of it are swallowed into the golem and the distortion of the golem's face as the clay that it is made of is displaced by the man's face. In the final of three images from this perspective, both the man and golem are ostensibly faceless.

The perspective pulls back. Though they are merged at the head, the rest of their bodies remain distinct. A clear depiction of the man's flaccid penis indicates there has been no penetration.

Then, over the next sequence of panels, the man's entire body is pulled into the golem.

Suddenly we are with the man, presumably inside the golem. He is surrounded on all sides by earth that is run through with plant roots and worms. His eyes, which are closed in the first of the inside-the-golem panels, open in the next. In the third, he looks calm. In the fourth, he looks panicked. In the fifth, he opens his mouth. In the sixth, he screams.

The golem explodes. Clumps of moist earth fly outward from the bed, striking the walls of the room. The largest clump strikes the grandfather clock. Over several panels, it slides from the face of the clock down the clock's body and to the floor[13].

In the last panel of the issue, the perspective overhead, the man is lying on his back on the bed, staring at the ceiling. His eyes are sterile. He is alone. The sound of the grandfather clock chiming fills the air around him.

Notes

---

[1] Last night, I had what had to have been a panic attack. I can't think of what else to call it. I suddenly became concerned that I was a golem that Kellan had created and that this comic series had been written not for the reasons previously suspected but because Kellan, in the wake of Natalie's death, feeling guilty about the secret he was keeping from me, had devised it as a means of making me aware of the truth. It was a short-lived episode, lasting only a half an hour or so. Afterwards, I called Egret and told her about it. She wondered if it might have been an expression of the grief I feel over Kellan's disappearance[1a].

[1a] She encouraged me to include things like this in these footnotes. She says the story of who Kellan is seems incomplete without them.

[2] The food is once again amorphous.

[3] I'm not sure how else to describe them. They don't follow any regular curve. They looked to me like lines that are anxious about being straight.

[4] Kellan claims to see auras (I use the word "claims" only because what someone else sees is an unconfirmable phenomenon; I have no reason to doubt him). He says specifically that he sees what he interprets as little bits of writing scribbled into the space just outside a person's skin, not at all times but sometimes[4a].

[4a] For a better understanding of the phenomena, see the people in the land of Uf, visited by Otello during the first of his three quests (the Southward/Downward Quest), all of whom are surrounded by words that they have learned to conjure in the air around them[4b].

[4b] Now that I think of it, the irregular lines that I describe in note 3 as anxious resemble words that are not fully formed.

[5] When Natalie and Kellan first met, Natalie told him she sometimes felt "apart of things."[5a]. Kellan was initially confused, unable to reconcile what he had heard, "I sometimes feel a part of things," with her sad tone. When they eventually sorted out the confusion, Kellan attempted to correct Natalie, explaining to her that the correct phrase should be "apart from things."[5b] Natalie was annoyed that Kellan's takeaway from what she considered to be a moment of vulnerability

had been grammatical. From that point forward, she used the phrase "apart of things" as often as she could in his presence.

[5a] A phrase she learned from her grandmother, who was not a native English speaker, though I can't remember where she was from or if I ever knew.

[5b] The phrase was not something that Natalie said often around other people. In fact, it was something that she had only ever said around her grandmother, who, as is my understanding, had never said it around anyone but Natalie, in whom she had confided a certain existential despair that she'd kept hidden from everyone else. Because of this, no one had ever had the chance to correct Natalie; until Kellan, it had been one of those linguistic solipsisms that all of us are prone to.

[6] For me at least, Moosipher always calls to mind the dark parking lot scene in *Tramplemundus* where Christopher, aka The Edge Perfect (the most powerful man in the world and one-time leader of The Carnival of Crusaders), who at the beginning of the series single-handedly saves the world from an interdimensional invasion, now drunk after a holiday party, is prodded into a petty fist fight by and with the guy hired to wear the Moosipher costume for the Christmas season. Part of the reason I have this response, and what most people don't know, is that even though Moosipher figures into the Munduson universe in a variety of ways, Kellan created the mascot specifically for the purpose of this single scene, which he knew from the moment of the series's inception would be the awful anti-climax of Christopher's story.

[7] This quote is a reference to *The Caligo*, a fictional comic series that Kellan never included in any of his works but talked about with his friends and during his appearances at conventions. The series, according to Kellan, is part of the Nexus universe, a comic book universe created by Franklin Farley, the arch-nemesis that Kellan invented for himself when he first started making comics[7a].

[7a] I am not quite sure that I am equipped to explain this particular Kellan peculiarity. I can say only that both Farley's life and comic book universe seem to have been imagined by Kellan in such extensive detail that he could speak of it with a casualness that the rest of us are only capable of when we speak of something real (for a long while, I suspected that Kellan had a secret stash of notes regarding Farley,

sketches of the vast realm the non-existent man occupied, but Kellan insisted otherwise and no such stash of notes has ever been found). As for what Farley and his universe represent, I would say that he's Kellan's version of the bureaucratic everyman, king of the status quo, producing comics that promote the opiating values Kellan associates with docility of the human spirit. He is, according to Kellan's sometimes venomous accounts, a propaganda machine disguised as an artist, a traitor to the creative forces pushing back against the viral mediocrity that, in Kellan's view, threatens to rob living of life and make the future uninhabitable.

[8] Knowing Kellan as I do, it is highly likely that, though he did not record them in the comics, he imagined thoroughly each of the golem iterations indicated by these sticks; experienced for himself the man's unique struggle with each of the golems that the reader only presumes are buried in the backyard.

[9] When we were children, Kellan used to amuse himself at my expense by passing me notes in class that contained cartoon images in which one character was saying something to another character through a speech bubble that was blocked[9a]. It amused him because it drove me crazy. I always wanted desperately to know what the characters were saying, being sure that what they were saying was important enough for Kellan to have gone to such lengths to share it. Kellan, of course, knew better; knew that the obfuscation was the point and it delighted him to watch me struggle. I bring this up because I believe that here, with this scene, it is Kellan himself who is the butt of the joke, the one who desperately wants to know what is being said. Whether he sees himself as playing that role voluntarily or if he feels like a victim I can't say. Both possibilities make sense here, the former as a product of guilt, the latter as a product of despair.

[9a] As time went on, he found increasingly clever ways to integrate the obfuscation into the scene taking place, the most clever being a tactic inspired by the window of our local comic book store: the two characters in the note were standing inside a comic shop, visible through the glass storefront which had painted on it a comic book character that was saying something through a speech bubble, which speech bubble was a) almost directly in front of the speech bubble

carrying what the character inside the store was saying to the other (several of the inside speech bubble's curved edges were visible poking out from behind the outside bubble's edges) and b) empty, waiting to be filled in by the artist of the window mural who was standing to the side of the bubble, out of the way of what was visible inside the store, with paint brush raised.

[10] Though given the events of the past few issues, I have trouble viewing this as anything but discomfort, and, in fact, have only included excitement as a possibility at the insistence of Egret, who after years and years of editing Kellan's work, feels that all ambiguities should be noted.

[11] Or the bed, says Egret. This is true. The man could be moving toward the bed and not the woman. In fact, despite what physics might have to say about it, he could be moving away from the woman as he moves toward the bed. To quote Finas, the subterranean janitor-turned-"healer" from *The Mall Beasts:* "Such is the hard-to-quantify complexity of the human condition.[11a]"

[11a] Of course, Finas says this before extracting someone's tooth with a pair of pliers and does so at the end of a contemplation on why people fear her in her relatively benign capacity as a dentist more than in her much more morbid capacity as a physician, but I think it still works here.

[12] Bearing no resemblance to a lemon.

[13] Mirroring the final scene in Issue 2.

Issue 10

Cover: Same as previous, but the moon is now blocked by a silhouette of the golem's head as it leans over to look in the hole.

Summary:

The issue is a single large page folded into normal-comic-book-page sized quarters and placed between the unattached folded cover sheet. The panels on the page (once it is unfolded[1]) are nested:

The man, in a non-descript t-shirt, is holding with his right hand and looking at a piece of paper[2] on which there is a drawing of the man in the suit he was wearing in the first issue (though here it isn't wet)[3], a wedding band on the fourth finger of his left hand, holding with his right hand and looking at a piece of paper on which there is a drawing of him with a woman (her face is obscured by a combination of the angle of her head's downward tilt and her hair), the two of them dressed in casual daily attire, she an engagement ring and a wedding band on the fourth finger of her left hand, holding between them (each of them holding one of the lateral edges with the hands of their outer arms, i.e. she with the left, he with the right) and looking at a piece of paper on which there is a drawing of the man and the woman (her face is obscured), wearing Hawaiian shirts and leis, she with an engagement ring and a wedding band on the fourth finger of the holding hand, holding between them (lateral edges, outer arms) and looking at a piece of paper on which there is a drawing of the man and the woman (her face obscured), she in a wedding dress, he in a tuxedo, she with an engagement ring on the fourth finger of the holding hand, holding between them (lateral edges, etc…) and looking at a piece of paper on which there is a drawing of the man and the woman (face obscured), in casual attire, she with an engagement ring on the fourth finger of the holding hand, holding between them (lateral edges, etc.…) and looking at a piece of paper on which there is a drawing of the man and the woman (face obscured), in baseball jerseys[4] (she, a Kalamazoo Clothespins jersey, he, a Christchurch Circusfreaks shirt[5]), holding between them (lateral edges, etc.…) and looking at a piece of paper on which there is a drawing of the man and the woman (face obscured), in Halloween costumes[6] (she a bumble bee, he a lion[7]), holding between them (lateral edges, etc.…) and looking at a piece of paper on which there is a drawing of the man and the woman (face obscured), in safari attire[8], holding between them (lateral edges, etc.…) and looking at a piece of paper on which there is a drawing of the man and the woman (face obscured)…[9]…a piece of paper on which there is a drawing of the man, in casual attire, holding with his right hand but not looking at—here the man is suddenly looking away from the paper he holds and up, it seems, at the man and woman who hold the paper that holds him—a piece of paper on which…[10,11]

Notes

---

[1] To avoid all confusion, the folding was purely for the sake of fitting the page between the normal-sized front and back covers. The entirety of the image that follows is contained on a single side of the folded paper, was created prior to the folding, and is not disturbed nor enhanced in any way by the folding. For the sake of apprehending it, one can assume that no folds exist and need only appreciate that it is sixteen times larger than a normal comic book page.

[2] The piece of paper is located at the center of the image[2a] and the man toward the right side[2b] so that the only part of him obstructing any of the paper is his hand, which holds the paper at its edge.

[2a] The pieces of paper in subsequent images are also located at the center of those images.

[2b] And the man in subsequent images is always located toward the right side.

[3] I briefly returned to the first issue to confirm my suspicion.

[4] Natalie, after they had been dating for almost half a year, challenged Kellan to take her on his idea of a "normal" date, and so, he took her to the first of only two baseball games he has ever been to in his life.

[5] The two "dream" teams from *Clothespins and Circuses*, the baseball teams that played each other every single night in Madge McGuinty's dreams.

[6] I'm presuming that the costumes indicate Halloween. The couple could be wearing costumes for some other reason, however unlikely that is.

[7] Kellan and Natalie came to my annual Halloween party each year dressed as a lion and a bumblebee (which supports my assumption in the previous footnote), though they alternated who wore which. This was a joke that they enjoyed, the fact that two artists would resort to something so mundane and routine on the one day of the year when American creativity is permitted to bloom. The switching, because it pretended to challenge assumptions, made the joke funnier to them (and has also made it impossible for me to remember with certainty

which costumes the man and woman are wearing in this issue; it is conceivable that I have recalled them in reverse).

[8] It's possible that the two are in costume here as well, though it seems unlikely.

[9] A dozen or so iterations exist here, but the differences between them become increasingly subtle, a fact complicated by the successive size reductions (had I had more time[9a], it might have been possible to study each image and access the distinctions). My recollections/ability to interpret them consequently became/is now limited, and after discussing it, Egret and I have agreed that my conjectures would not be worth more than the reader simply knowing that further iterations exist in this space and that each of those iterations contain both the man and the woman.

[9a] (and foreknowledge of the disappearances)

[10] The images go on beyond this, but this was the final image that I, even with the glasses, was able to make out with any reasonable certainty. Already by this point, Kellan was accomplishing something impossible re: the detail to size ratio (this final image was approximately the size of Abraham Lincoln's head on a penny), and how he managed to continue on successfully, I do not know.

[11] This comes to mind: In *The Digit*, 1 has access to a single book that he finds in his chamber. From time to time, we see pages in this book, one of which pages says the following: "Before we see ourselves, we see ourselves in everything. Before we see the truth, we see ourselves."

ISSUE 11

Cover: Same as previous, but now the golem's shadowy hand extends into the hole toward the bottom.

Summary[1]:

The man sits at the dining room table. Across from him sits a clay child, about six years old. Between them: a box of Marshmallow Ka-Pows[2]. Before them: two bowls. The man wears jeans and a t-shirt. The clay child wears a pink child's nightgown, a galaxy mark visible on her left cheek. The man is watching the clay child intently as she eats spoonful after spoonful of the cereal without looking up. The perspective closes in on and then shifts around the clay child's cereal consumption: panel by panel: the clay child bringing the spoon to her face, the mouth opening, the jaw chewing, the spoon dipping down into the milk, a glistening trail of snot running from the nose toward the upper lip, the mouth closing down on the spoon, the spoon in mid-flight carrying a small heap of cereal (a single marshmallow cube riding atop it), the clay child's fingers curled around the handle of the spoon[3]. The perspective shifts outward again to include both the man and the clay child. The clay child looks up from the cereal and sees the man looking at her. The man sticks his tongue out at her. The clay child's face swells as she tries to hold in a laugh. Close-up: the clay child's mouth and nose as milk shoots out of it[4]. The clay child is disturbed by this. The man, recognizing her distress, leans forward toward his bowl. Close-up: the man's nose at the edge of the milk in his cereal bowl (the cereal has already been eaten, but the milk contains a few small specks of spongey milk-soaked wheat bits). Full room: the man snorts some milk into his nose. He looks up from the bowl. His face is contorted (from the pain of bringing milk into his sinuses). The clay child stares at him in disbelief. "It goes both ways," he says. "Isn't that amazing?" The clay child begins to laugh again. The man's face relaxes, and he laughs too.

The scene shifts to one of the house's bathrooms. They stand before a mirror, she on a stool, he behind her. The backs of their bodies are visible in the foreground; in the background, in the mirror, the front sides of their heads, necks and portions of their torsos. Her left arm is lifted and bent, her elbow out to the side at a right angle to her body, her left hand holding a toothbrush in front of her open mouth. The man is reaching over her left shoulder with his left arm, his left hand cupped around her left hand, his right hand resting on her right shoulder. In the mirror, he sees her eyes looking up at the reflection of his eyes in the mirror[5]. "Do I have to?" he says. She nods vigorously. He begins to sing (denoted by little musical notes): "Every tooth / is a piece of the truth / so keep them white / and a beautiful sight..." As he does this, he, like a puppeteer, helps her brush her teeth. "When you lie / your molars die. / Telling fibs / makes your teeth and also your ribs / sad sad sad sad sad..."

A shift again to a seemingly unfamiliar room in the house[6]: a child's bedroom (child-sized bed, pushed into a corner, adorned in cupcake covered sheets and matching duvet; painted on the wall over the bed, Moosipher; painted on the adjacent wall, a doo-chim[7]; an adult-sized captain's chair to the left of the bed). The man and clay child stand next to an adult-sized dresser. The clay child, now wearing only a pair of children's underwear[8], points to the middle of five drawers. The man opens the drawer and pulls out a pink dress. The clay child shakes her head. The man puts the dress back and pulls out a blue one. The clay child nods. Then she raises both arms over her head. The man puts the dress on over them and pulls it down so that it sits properly on the clay child's body.

The man and the clay child go to a park. They stroll along a concrete pathway. The man keeps pointing to birds and naming them. The clay child, at first, repeats the names of the birds, but as the walk progresses, she grows increasingly interested in chasing them. The man tries to prevent this, corralling the clay child back to his side as she drifts away from him. Eventually, though, she runs off after a bird, and he is forced to chase her. She is fast, and he has more difficulty than expected catching up to her. The chase ends when the clay child, consumed with excitement, leaps into the air, seemingly of the belief that she can fly. She is so convinced of this, in fact, that she is unprepared for the ground she approaches, landing harshly on the front side of her torso without bracing herself in any way.

As the man arrives where the clay child is lying, he pauses for a moment. For one panel, he stands over her, between actions[9]; the bird that she was attempting to fly after now a black spot hanging in the sky above them like a star. Then he picks her up off the ground. He turns her around and holds her in his arms. She is crying. "Are you hurt?" he says. "Are you ok?" "I can't fly," she says through her tears. "I think I'm broken." The man laughs. "You're not broken," he says. "No one can fly." "Why not?" says the clay child. "Because we aren't built that way," says the man. "Why aren't I built that way?" says the clay child.

After that, there are four blank panels and the issue ends[10].

Notes

---

[1] It's worth noting that there's no indication of how much time has passed between the previous issues and this one. In fact, there's no real indication of how much total time has elapsed between the first issue of the series and this one[1a].

[1a] Kellan never cares about time in his works (much to the chagrin of Egret). There is linearity and a-linearity of events, but duration is always a murky feature. He feels that people relate better to the changes in the size of an emotion, as it grows larger or smaller, than they do to the passage of time, and that where that change is portrayed in enough detail, people will apprehend momentum, the life-affirming facet of any literary event, even if there's no duration.

[2] The frosted wheat cereal with jam-filled marshmallow cubes that Daniel, alter-ego of Polygon Two, becomes addicted to in *Tramplemundus*. It's also featured in *Brine Comedy* (in her madness, Verunica serves hot bowls of it to guests in her restaurant as soup), *The Mall Beasts* (the tunnel denizens stockpile the marshmallow cubes after discovering the cubes' surprising and inexplicable flammability), *Crustacean Wedding* (members of the *Club Orgasmic* uses it to power themselves up during the orgy sequence), and *Punching Bag* (Wick is seen eating it for dinner in his dingy apartment on the first page of the series).

[3] The point here, I think, is to illustrate the clay child's disconcerting obliviousness to being watched by the man (and by us, who are made uncomfortable by the absence of any defense against our intrusion, who are made uncomfortable by such intense innocence, such intense lack of protocolled invulnerability). Or the clay child's intense joy, her sense that everything is right in the universe and that rightness unassailable, which produces the obliviousness. Or our struggle as adults to see one without the other. Or Kellan's specific struggle with the adulthood that led him to the turn he takes here.

[4] The close-up drained all the charm from the moment for me, supplanting it with grossness. I think Kellan did this almost as a way to say that while we as readers can intellectually appreciate the existence

of joy in that moment, the moment itself and the joy it contains aren't for us; that it doesn't matter if we appreciate the joy or not because it is happening for the man and the clay child[4a].

[4a] Kellan has an issue with people's belief that they need to be part of something outside for corresponding somethings inside to matter. He feels that mass media conditions us to seek validation for our emotions from some consensus[4b], which leads him to be both protective of his own emotions (he does not like it when people have indirect emotional responses to his emotional responses, i.e. when he once caught someone smiling at him and Natalie kissing (several days of ranting and ranting about the ignominy of it)) and outspoken about people abdicating power over their emotions to others (he does not like it when people ask him how he intended for one of his works to make them feel)[4c].

[4b] a theme he explores rather on-the-nosedly in *Ratio of Sanity*, where Escovailia has replaced its court system with a body that instead of governing moral right and wrong, governs appropriateness of having an emotion.

[4c] He's always complaining to me about how modern entertainment, meaning mostly movies and television, is comprised almost exclusively of emotional cues that have no foundation, that they function entirely on the premise that everyone comes to them seeking to be in agreement with them. One of the most quoted lines in any of his works is what *Crustacean Wedding's* Tank, the guru who leads the self-liberation workshop that Marjorie attends after she discovers Marco's unfaithfulness to the love triangle, says to the workshop's attendees. "Are the people on TV acting like you," he says, "or are you acting like the people on TV?" This line captures perfectly Kellan's fear that people are no longer generating their own emotions internally but receiving them from broadcasts (material and psychic), or that they're no longer able to determine what is from within and what is being implanted.

[5] Not the first time Kellan has engaged such a subtle convolution. My personal favorite scene in *The Mall Beasts* is when Jasper and Ursula, the two love-stuck teenagers, separated inside the mirror maze that Stanley has assembled from discarded public restroom mirrors, stop searching for each other and just stare into the reflections of each other's eyes. This was also Natalie's favorite scene, which annoyed Kellan, for

whom the scene, in the context of the work's scope, was of middling importance. He spent considerable efforts trying to convince her to select a different favorite, suggesting the earthquake scene or the scene in which Duncan, out of spite, toils relentlessly toward the invention of a toilet powerful enough to flush waste upward toward the surface dwellers, but Natalie insisted that nothing could trump the way that Kellan had so gracefully captured the sweet, convoluted innocence of young love.

[6] It's possible that this is one of the rooms from the first issue reconfigured for the clay child, and I found it frustrating that I could not determine whether or not this was the case. I felt that the transformation of one of the rooms in the house into this new room would possess an important symbolism that I (and other readers) want access to. But Kellan established the nebulosity of the house at the outset, so there must be some reason that as we arrive here this detail is obscured by it.

[7] One of the mythical creatures that the subterranean denizens in *The Mall Beasts* discover as they build their tunnels deeper into the earth. It's sort of a birdgoat that salivates a silky substance with enormous tensile strength, a substance that Roger uses to make hammocks.

[8] There was a pattern on the underwear, but it was too small to comprehend unaided and I did not feel comfortable examining them with the glasses.

[9] It might be that the amount of time passing between panels is much less than I am assuming it to be and that Kellan was only capturing a moment in the sequence of moments that constitute the man's continuous actions, a moment that only seems like the man is in a paused position because Kellan has cleverly taken it out of context so that we could observe it.

[10] It is here that the blank panels begin. They appear a few other times throughout what remains of the series (I will continue to note them in the summaries). Sometimes, it's only a single panel. Sometimes, it's several in a row[10a].

[10a] I've thought about them a fair amount since my one read through. My initial conclusion was that Kellan had left these panels blank to hide

something from either the reader or himself. This is an interpretation that I encourage readers to explore, as it seems quite plausible. But there are other possibilities that I have conceived of over time: that these panels are not blank but contain material that I was unable to perceive at the time[10b], that these panels had once contained material that had been erased from the parchment using some chemical process[10c], or that these panels were left blank so that someone else could fill them in at some point[10d].

[10b] Maybe these panels were rendered in an ink that only appears under a blacklight or at some temperature that was unavailable while I was reading the issues.

[10c] Kellan could have decided after the fact that he wanted to hide whatever he had put there, perhaps because whatever it was had exposed something he himself hadn't known about the existence of until it was on the page but which had he known of it beforehand he would have wanted to keep hidden; or maybe he'd always intended to erase whatever it was, had decided in advance the expression of it was enough for him, that the satisfaction he sought was independent of the recognition of these elements by other parties; and in either case, the question remains as to why he would have chosen to erase instead of burying the page and starting over.

[10d] Egret has tearfully called this the "Natalie's Ghost" theory.

ISSUE 12

Cover: Same as previous, but now a human hand reaches up toward the hand the golem has extended into the hole.

Summary:

Opens with an aerial view of a suburban neighborhood. It is just possible to discern the houses and gatherings of trees, a few colored specks that are probably cars, and some swimming pools. Over the course of several panels, the view telescopes downward toward the street level. In each of these panels, the details of one small area come into greater clarity. It gradually becomes possible to make out the individual trees, the makes of the cars, and colored specks that, given their numbers and colors and placement, must be people[1]. Eventually, the view comes to rest directly above an area that represents less than 1/100th of the total area seen in the first panel[2]. The man is standing in the grass between a strip of sidewalk and the road. Colored bits of confetti surround him, though the absence of any festivities indicate they are from something that occurred previously[3]. The view shifts so that he is visible from the front. He looks up the road to the left and then back to center. He looks at his watch. He looks up the road to the left and back to the center again. He looks up the road to the left. The view shifts to his perspective: road down the middle of the view, running up over a hill at the horizon, nothing on it, surrounded on both sides by generic suburban patterning (sidewalk, grass, unnaturally placed trees). The top of a school bus appears over the horizon. The rest of the school bus follows.

A sequence of three panels (view from the road): 1. the man standing on the curb again 2. a bus stopped in front of where the man was, obscuring him 3. the man standing on the curb, next to him the clay child, both of them facing the road[4].

The man and clay child walk home. The man asks the clay child what she did in school. The clay child says, "We learned some words." The man says, "Which words?" The clay child says, "I don't know. I forget." The man says, "You forgot?" The clay child says, "They weren't very good ones. I like other words better, so I'll just remember those words. It'll be fine." The man says, "Oh, will it?" The clay child says, "Yes, daddy. You're being silly." The clay child stops walking. "Daddy," she says, "is tonight a Window Eyes night?" The man picks the clay child up. "No," he says. "Tonight is a different story." "Oh," says the clay child, "I'm worried though." "About what?" says the man. "Well," says the clay child, "what if something happens to Window Eyes or Glass Man and we aren't there to see it?" The man laughs. "That can't happen," he says. "Why not?" says the clay child. "That's not how stories work," says the man. "They only happen *when* we see them. They need us." The clay child puts a finger to her cheek, like she is contemplating. She closes her eyes. She opens them. "I can see them now," she says. "Does that mean they are happening?"

Two blank panels[5].

The man and the clay child are eating dinner in the living room, in front of the television. On the screen: cartoon images. They are eating Marshmallow Ka-Pows again[6]. They sit like this for a full page of panels, the passage of time exhibited through their eating motions and the changes in the blurry images on the television. Then the clay child looks at the man and says, "I think I'm getting sleepy." "Are you sure?" the man says. "It's still early." "That's ok," says the clay child, "I think it's time for me to go to bed." "Ok," says the man. He takes the clay child's cereal bowl from her. "You go upstairs and get ready," he says. The clay child runs from the room. When she is gone, the man turns off the television. He picks up the bowls.

The man in the kitchen, putting the bowls in the sink.

The man in his study, at his desk. He opens one of the drawers and pulls out a handful of pages.

Upstairs, in the clay child's bedroom, the man sits in the captain's chair. The clay child is in bed, underneath the covers. The man reads to her from the pages. "Verunica was distraught," the man says. "What's distraught?" the clay child says. "It means upset," the man says. "Like sad?" says the clay child. "It's more than just sad," the man says. "It's like sad *and* confused at the same time." The clay child thinks. "I'm distraught sometimes," she says. "Like in school when they don't have enough milk for everyone and I don't get one." "Exactly," says the man. "Should I continue?" The clay child nods. "Verunica was distraught," the man says[7]. "She decided to go for a walk. She walked along the road that led to her house, but when she got to her home, she decided to keep walking. She walked and walked, for almost an hour until she found herself in a part of town that she hadn't been to recently. It had changed so much since she was last there, she barely recognized it. Everything was bright and colorful, and all the stores had strange names. The Ghost in the Pearl, Boutique Boutique Boutique, Stars and Krunkle. She couldn't tell from these names what any of these stores was selling, which only made her more distraught." The clay child interrupted. "Why did this make her more distraught?" A panel of silence. "I'm not sure," says the man. "Maybe it's because she wants things to be easy to understand and none of these stores are." "But can't she just go in and ask the people inside what the stores are?" says the clay child. "She could," says the man, "but I don't think that she's upset about the stores being hard to understand. I think she's upset about other stuff that's hard to understand." "Like what stuff?" says the clay child. "Stuff that she can't go inside of," says the man, "stuff she can't ask people about." "Like what?" says the clay child. A panel of silence. A second panel of silence. "Like her feelings, maybe," says the man. "But I ask you about my feelings all the time," says the clay child. "It's different," says the man. "These are adult feelings." "Why can't she ask people about adult feelings?" says the clay child. "Because it doesn't work that way," says the man. "Why not?" says the clay child. "Because it doesn't," says the man. "Because it doesn't why?" says the clay child. A panel of silence. "If you keep asking questions," the man says, "we won't get to the end of the story. Do you want to get to the end?" A panel of silence. "Ok," says the clay child. The man continues: "Eventually Verunica went into a store called Broc and

Brats, which turned out to be a hip food establishment that offered a limited menu of high-end broccoli and hot dog items[8]. She looked around at the décor, the broccoli and hot dog murals on the wall, examined the menu, its eight lonely items. She shook her head. 'We spend our entire lives,' she thought, 'trying to create the perfect childhood for ourselves.[9]'"

In the next panels, the man continues to read, but his speech bubbles are filled only with straight lines. The focus of these panels is the clay child's eyelids, which slowly slide down over her eyes until she is asleep. At that point, the man stands up and exits the room, turning off the lights as he goes.

Notes

____

[1] Technically, the colored specks that are people are identical to the colored specks that were, from the much greater height, cars. I had the foresight to double check this while reading this issue.

[2] This is an imprecise estimate that I've made here purely to make the effect more concrete for those who have not seen the material firsthand.

[3] The colored specks here are also identical to the specks that once were people and cars. In fact, in all three instances, the specks seem to occur at the same locations in the panels (if you laid the three panels that contain the identical specks on top of one other, the specks would align perfectly).

[4] They look like two people in a police lineup, which is, given this scenario, an unrealistic position. There's no reason that the clay child and man would stand in that position after the clay child gets off the bus. Perhaps Kellan is being cinematic, in which case this would be him making another joke; however, that seems out of place in this moment, even in this semi-nebulous world he has created. It is more likely that he decided to portray them this way so that he could see them together, stripped of function, to determine their worth to him, in which case he was probably at this point starting to doubt whether he wanted to go on. I can imagine him staring at this panel for hours or days, catatonic in appearance, but enormously active internally, seeking an answer (specifically here a reason for him to continue, an angle, a hope, a vision), a position I have seen him in countless times[4a,4b].

[4a] He did this often in our first grade class, would stare at some object in the room with such intensity, oblivious to the teacher's call of his name, freaking her out, freaking me out, freaking everyone out; and when he realized how much it disturbed people, he started to do it just for amusement, a thing it took me a little while to figure out, though I, to this day, cannot always tell when he is doing it for fun and when he is actually transfixed on a contemplation.

[4b] He did this with a photo of Natalie after first meeting her, just stared at the photo for eight hours in my living room[4c]. He told me later that he had, after great struggle, broken her down to a simple set of

understandings. He did not explain why he had done this or to what purpose he would put what he had discovered or what those understandings were. Nor did he ever admit to me how impossibly wrong those understandings had been, though he did admit to her on their first day that he had broken her down in such a way, which Natalie, as she would explain to me later, found adorable, for reasons that she did not explain to me, thinking, I suppose, that I, having known Kellan for so long, would understand.

[4c] I have become accustomed to the phenomenon of Kellan sitting like a stone in the center of my living spaces since he often chooses to do this in my home, I think because on some level the depth of contemplation scares even him and it's comforting for him to know that I'm around to pull him out if he gets lost within himself, though were that to happen, I have no idea how I would do that.

[5] Let's say that the panels aren't blank, that they're rendered in some kind of "invisible" ink. The question then is why would Kellan have done this? Is this him speaking quite coarsely to what it feels like to lose someone you love, not an emptiness or an erasure but a presence that is indetectable?

[6] Any time these two are eating, they are eating Marshmallow Ka-Pows, which is 100% Kellan, who as a child only wanted to eat sugary cereals (Sharon tried to prevent this and was mostly unsuccessful). Even as an adult, Kellan wanted to eat sugary cereal all the time and did, seven to ten boxes a week, until Natalie came along and put a stop to it.

[7] A small thought bubble hovers to the left of the clay child as the man reads her the story. Inside it, tiny images of what is being recounted[7a], a comic inside a comic[7b].

[7a] Initially, I used the glasses to view them, but the images proved simplistic enough that I was ultimately able to make out what they were intended to be with my naked eye in conjunction with what the man was saying.

[7b] I considered including this in the main text, but the bubble felt like a footnote to what the man was saying. In fact, it hung next to the man's speech bubble where a footnote would be placed relative to a word. Placing mention of it here seemed truer to the experience.

[8] Kellan on hot dogs and broccoli: "They're the love and hate of food items in America. Americans are expected, if they want to fit in, to love hot dogs, which they should want to eat any chance they can, and hate broccoli, which they must eat to be healthy but only after some struggle."

[9] This story seems to be from the *Brine Comedy* universe but isn't a story that appeared in any issues of that series. It's either an outtake or something new that Kellan decided to add here[9a]. Regardless of which, I can't place it into the series timeline; I don't know if it's supposed to take place before or after Verunica's nervous breakdown, whether what is happening is supposed to indicate the onset of some crisis or if it is something that occurs in the exhaustion she likely experiences after one.

[9a] All the stories that Kellan reads to the clay child, except for *Window Eyes and Glass Man*, are from his comic universes, all of them either outtakes or new additions.

ISSUE 13

Cover: In the hole, a close-up of the hand from the bottom clasping the hand from the top.

Summary:

The golem[1] sits in the front yard of the house. The view is from behind her, facing the house[2]. She is doing something with her arms and hands that is obscured by her small body. A bird walks around the lawn, occasionally pecking at the ground. Eventually, it finds a worm and flies away with the worm in its beak.

The man sits in the kitchen, reading a book[3]. A voice from around the corner intrudes. "Daddy," the voice says, "I made you something." The golem enters the kitchen holding something in her hands. She approaches the man and holds her hands out. Close-up on her hands: a somewhat circular brown patty sits in her palms. "What is it?" says the man. "Don't be silly, Daddy," the golem says. "You know what it is." "I don't know," says the man. "It's a pie," says the golem. "What kind of pie?" says the man. "It's a mud pie!" says the golem. The man appears alarmed by this. He stands and picks the golem from the floor. He spins her around, inspecting her entire body. The golem squeals with delight, an indication that she believes this to be some sort of aerial ride. The man puts her down. "Where did you get the mud?" he says. "From the ground," the golem says. The man expresses visible relief. Though she did not notice the alarm, the golem notices the relief.

"What's wrong?" she says. "Nothing," says the man. "I had a stupid thought." The golem laughs. "You have a lot of stupid thoughts," she says. Before the man can react, the golem taps him on the shoulder. "You're it," she says and runs off. The man, alone in the kitchen, looks at his hands. Close-up of his hands[4]: his palms are empty. The golem calls out to him as he continues to look at his hands. "I said *you're it*!" she says. The man looks up. He runs off after her.

The man sits at his desk in the study, writing on a sheet of paper in front of him. He crosses something out and then continues writing. He puts the pen in his mouth and chews on it. He writes some more. He puts the pen down, picks up the paper and puts it into one of the drawers of the desk.

Dinner on the couch. The golem throws a marshmallow at the man. The man throws a marshmallow at the golem.

The man pulls a marshmallow from between the couch cushions, the golem now absent.

The man retrieves the pages from the desk drawer.

The man sits in the captain's chair in the golem's room. The golem is in bed beneath the covers. In the first panel of this sequence, the man reads from the pages. "Window Eyes is missing," he says. In the next panel, the man continues to read[5]; in a thought bubble attached to the golem, what the man says is translated into imagery[6]: a man made of glass, in a ballerina's outfit (complete with tutu), stands in a laboratory, frantic look on his face, a thought bubble attributed to him inside of which is a woman with brown hair and blue eyes wearing a ballerina's outfit (complete with tutu) and a pair of glasses made from two small window frames attached to wire or plastic arms[7].

The panel after that is entirely a thought bubble (the edges of the panel itself have the cloud-like quality of thought bubbles; extending from the bottom left corner into the void space of the page are three small circles of increasingly smaller size). The images inside it are not of the room the man and the golem are in but of the room that is the golem's imagination: "It has to have been Dire Rhombus," says Glassman. "He's been trying to get his hands on her for years." The subsequent panels continue to take place in thought bubbles. "I can track him through the Swarm Feed," says Glassman. He enters a room containing a large beehive. "Opening the portal," says Glassman. "Releasing the swarm." He presses a button on the beehive. A swarm of bees erupts from the top of it. The bees cluster in front of him. He shows them a picture. Close-up on the picture: a green troll wearing a top hat, holding a gun in his right hand. "Please find him," says Glassman. "Find him as fast as you can."[8] The bees leave. Glassman remains in the beehive room alone. A light from above casts his shadow onto the floor. Glassman looks at his shadow. He raises his arm, and the arm of his shadow moves. He spreads his fingers, and the fingers of his shadow spread. He bends his index finger, and the shadow's index finger disappears into the shadow's hand. He looks at the shadow of his hand, at the space where the finger was. A single bee returns. "We have found Dire Rhombus," it says. "Take me to him!" says Glassman. Glassman and the bee cross through three rooms: the laboratory, a bedroom, and a kitchen. They arrive in a garage[9], which contains two adult-sized, children's-training-wheel-equipped bikes, one that is pink and one that is blue. Glassman pauses for a moment to look at the pink bike. Then he sits atop the blue bike and pedals toward the edge of the panel.

On the next page, Glassman rides the bike on the sidewalk in a suburban neighborhood[10], the bee flying in front of him. "This way," it says. "We are almost there." Glassman comes to an intersection. He carefully looks down the street to the right and down the street to the left.

A return to the golem's bedroom (the panels now have straight borders again): "Daddy," says the golem, "I have a question." The man looks up from the pages. "What is it?" he says. "You told me that Window Eyes and Glassman created Shay Doon, right?" "Yes," the man says, "they used magic to build a whole world called Shaidun so they could live there together." "But if they built it," the golem says, "why did they put the bad guys there?" A panel of silence. "I don't know," says the man. "Maybe... Yeah. I don't know."

Thought bubble panels (cloud-like edges): Glassman sits atop his bike in front of an ominous looking castle. He raises his arm like he did in the beehive room. He looks down and sees nothing but the enormous shadow of the castle. He leaps from the bike and races toward the castle entrance. He throws open the door. "Dire Rhombus," he screams. "Where are you?" He pauses for a moment. "Where is she?" he screams (the words are larger when he asks about Window Eyes, broaching the panel's edges and bleeding over into the void space slightly). Red-lettered cackling fills the panel, swirling around Glassman. He runs up a staircase, which leads him into a large throne room. Sitting on a throne is the troll-man from the picture that was shown to the bees. "Welcome," says Dire Rhombus. "To what do I owe the pleasure of this visit?" "Where is she?" Glassman shouts across the room (the words are not contained in a speech bubble; they fly across the room like throwing knives[11]). "I'm sure you mean that foul companion of yours?" says Dire Rhombus. "I have no idea." Glassman approaches the throne. "Don't lie to me," he says. "I know you've taken her." Dire Rhombus laughs. "I don't know what you're talking about." "I said don't lie to me," says Glassman. He stands before Dire Rhombus, thrusts his glass face into his adversary's troll snout. "Tell me where she is," he says, "tell me or I'll…" "You'll what?" says Dire Rhombus. "Break?" Glassman grabs Dire Rhombus by the collar of his shirt. "Tell me!" Dire Rhombus finally looks worried. "I don't know," he says. "I really don't. I haven't taken her." "Then who has?" "I don't know." Glassman lets go of Dire Rhombus. He turns from his foe. He falls to his knees. "Where are you?" he screams.

Outside the castle, these words fly through the air, knocking a bird from the purple sky.

Notes

---

[1] Egret and I feel that enough contextual distance has been created between the sequence of adult female golems and this young girl golem that I am comfortable referring to the girl as the golem, and she will be referred to as such from this point forward.

[2] The man might be visible through the house's front window. Using the glasses, it was possible to make out something in the house that resembled a person, but it was not clear enough for me to say confidently that it was him.

[3] Used the glasses to read the title. *The Rising Sun of Superland*, a book that Maryanne quotes from several times in *Maze on Dixon*. "This is a land that was once ruled by reason, now ruled by fear of boredom," she says in Issue 10, for instance. I don't think this quote relates to what's happening here in *Window Eyes*. It's just the first one I remembered.

[4] The close-up panels of the hands of the golem and the man are rendered in similitude. In both, the hands, palms face up, are pressed against each other along the pinky-side edges (like praying hands that have been butterflied open), the image as a whole presented so that the line where the pinky-edges join is along the hypotenuse that bisects the square shape of the panel (the fingertips towards the upper-right corner, the wrists toward the bottom left).

[5] The words are replaced here with lines.

[6] This thought bubble is significantly larger than the one that was associated with the golem in the previous issue (see Issue 12, note 7). It's about 1/5th the size of the half-page panel that contains it.

[7] This bubble is approximately the same size as the ones from the previous issue. I had to use the glasses to see the woman clearly.

[8] At first, I was surprised by the scripting here. It's an aping of pre-turn-of-the-century comic book scripting, which was overly simplistic and still mostly unaware, save for a few writers here and there, of the true artistic potential of the medium. This is the style that, as far as I understand, Frank Farley is imagined to have drawn his inspiration from when creating the Nexus Universe, and therefore one that Kellan (who drew his inspiration from those few pioneering writers) felt

disdain for. But having thought more about it, I have come to recognize what is actually happening here: this is a six-year old's interpretation of a story born from a grief so large that its bearer needed to create a surrogate who created a child to tell it to. The complexity of consciousness involved in this speaks to the difficulty of processing loss, mirrors even the layers of self that are thrown in the way of the agony to prevent it from running over the dream of life. And though it is convoluted, this is not a convolution of what Kellan was feeling; it is Kellan struggling to unrefract this experience.

[9] The garage is filled with garage-y things: old sports equipment, cans of paint, a garden hose, random power tools, and also a bucket like the one the man was using in the early issues during his initial attempts to create the golem (and in issue 0).

[10] A neighborhood that looks very much like the neighborhood portrayed in the previous issue.

[11] This image of the flying words seems to me to be beyond a six-year old's imagination, indicative therefore of a bleeding through of the master consciousness, which maybe wants to be closer to what is taking place?

Issue 14

Cover: In the hole, the hand and arm reaching up from the bottom hold on to the hand from the top, which is severed at the wrist from the arm that still extends down into the hole.

Summary:

Aerial view of a suburban neighborhood; in a small box in the upper right corner of this panel, it says: Temp: 91 degrees.

Scene at a playground: empty sandbox, empty swing set, unused slides, pigeons perched on the equipment and pecking at the sand.

Scene at a public pool: adults in bathing suits lie on lounge chairs beneath umbrellas while children in bathing suits run wildly around the pool or swim in it. A lifeguard sits in an elevated lifeguard chair at the center of this.

Exterior front of the man's house: the front door is closed. The front door opens. The man and the golem stand in the doorway. He wears shorts and a Hawaiian shirt, has a beach towel draped over his shoulders, black-framed sunglasses over his eyes, and a gym bag in hand. She wears a thin dress—the kind that a young child would wear over a bathing suit—also has on a pair of sunglasses (orange frames), holds a beach ball in her arms. They walk together across the front lawn, approach a car parked in front of the house, a blue, two-door convertible sedan with the top down. The man opens the passenger-side door, and the girl climbs into the backseat. The man fastens her seatbelt and proceeds around the car to the driver's side, opens the door, sits in the driver seat.

Aerial view from directly over the car: the man drives along a coastal road. Music notes surround the car. Perspective shift: in the car, the man sings (speech bubbles filled with musical notes, no words). The golem looks out toward the coast, into or across the ocean. The song stops. "How big is the ocean?" the golem says. "What?" says the man. He looks into the rearview mirror, sees the golem sitting in the backseat. "I said: How big is the ocean?" the golem says[1,2]. "It's most of the world," the man says. "How big is the world?" the golem says. "I don't know," says the man. "Sometimes it goes on forever and sometimes it just ends without warning." "Have you seen the whole thing?" the golem says. "I don't know how much I've seen," says the man. "Sometimes everything feels familiar and sometimes everything feels strange." "What's bigger?" says the golem, "the ocean or the place where we're going?" "The ocean is bigger than the beach," says the man. "What's bigger," says the golem, "the ocean or Shay Doon?" "I don't know," says the man. "How can we find out?" says the golem. "I don't know that either," says the man. "One day, I'm going to find out," says the golem. The man smiles.

The car pulls off the highway and stops at a booth that sits at the entrance to the destination. The man hands money to someone stationed in the booth and drives forward. The golem waves as they drive by. In the final panel of this sequence, we see into the booth, see the person in the booth looking impenetrable and exhausted[3].

The man parks the car, reaches back and unbuckles the golem. The man exits the vehicle first. As the golem is exiting, she drops the inflatable beach ball and the wind pushes it away from the car. The next dozen panels or so are from the "perspective" of the ball looking back on the golem as she sits in the car watching it, first as it rolls away and then as the man comes to retrieve it[4].

The man finds a spot on the crowded beach and lays out towels. The golem sits in the sand. The man applies sunscreen to himself. The golem begins building something with the sand. The man lies down on his towel, picks up a book and starts to read. The golem continues to build. A thought bubble appears over the golem's head containing an image of an office building/castle hybrid structure, more or less an office building flanked by two castle towers, with a drawbridge in the center of the building's lowest quarter. The thought bubble remains, the building image fixed while the golem continues to work on the sand structure. A single mound of sand grows in size but remains a mostly amorphous pile. The golem carves an upside-down "U" into the bottom of it. She creates two more amorphous piles next to the original pile. "Look, daddy," she says. "It's Window Eyes's headquarters." The man looks up from the book and at the piles. "That's great," he says. "Maybe Window Eyes is inside," says the golem. "I'm going to see." The golem slides her two hands, pressed together backside to backside, into the sand delineated by the upside-down "U" and then makes a spreading motion like one would make when opening a curtain. The sand pile collapses. "Nope," says the golem. "She's not here. Where is she?" The man continues to read. "Where is she, daddy?" the golem says. "Where is she?" "I don't know," says the man, still reading. The golem, unnoticed by the man, stands up and walks toward the ocean. She reaches the wet sand near the water's edge and stops. She stares.

In the next panels, the golem remains the focus, but the point from which she is viewed rises skyward. More of the beach and the people are visible around her, more of the ocean. As the elevation increases, the other people begin to vanish from the view until, in the final image of this sequence, there's just the tiny spec of the golem on the beach standing before an ocean that consumes the majority of the panel.

A jarring shift back to beach level, back specifically to the golem's feet in the sand. An ocean wave approaches and ends inches from her toes. The foot lifts. A step toward the remnants of that wave.

Before her foot touches the water, the man abruptly picks the golem off the sand from behind. He turns her around in his arms. He holds her so that they are face to face, his arms outstretched so he can look her in the eyes. He appears frantic. "What are you doing?" he says. "I want to go swimming," the golem says. "You can't go swimming," says the man. "Why not?" says the golem. "Because you don't know how," says the man. "Then I want to learn," says the golem. "You can't learn," says the man. "I can learn," says the golem. "You're not allowed," says the man[5]. "But what if that's where Window Eyes is?"

says the golem. "What if she's in the ocean?" "She's not in the ocean," says the man. "How do you know?" says the golem. "No one is in the ocean," says the man. "How do you know?" says the golem. "Because I'm a grownup and I know," says the man. The man continues to hold the golem at arm's length. They stare into each other's faces, the golem clearly angry, the man clearly buttressing himself against the glare of her displeasure. Neither of them speaks. A caption appears in a box in the lower right corner of a panel: "From that point on, the girl was ever fascinated with water." Another caption in the next panel: "And the man was ever more careful, particularly in the rain…" And in the next: "Particularly after the rain, for the girl could see herself in the mirror-slick surface of every puddle…"

A blank panel[6], followed by a sequence of panels in which, little by little, that blank space fills up with ocean water. The blank space becomes completely filled in the second to last panel of the issue. In the last panel, a beach ball is suspended in the water-filled panel's center.

Notes

¹ The words in the speech bubble are larger this time, indicating that the golem has elevated the volume of her voice so that the man can hear her speaking from the backseat.

² During this conversation, when the golem speaks, she is visible as a reflection in a close-up of the rearview mirror (the mirror takes up most of the panel: it is possible to see a small sliver of the windshield over the top and below the bottom of the mirror; the mirror itself is truncated on the sides so that only the middle 2/3rds of its total length are visible) [2a]. When the man speaks, we see him through the windshield of the car from an angle that positions the rearview mirror in front of the golem, blocking her out of the image entirely.

It should be noted that the golem's speech bubbles are also visible in the mirror. At first, it seems like they're merely in the car and laid over the mirror out of necessity, there being nowhere else convenient for Kellan to put them in the panel. But in one of the panels, the man places his hand on the mirror to adjust it slightly and when he does, one of his fingers obscures part of the bubble.

³ This is probably a "self-portrait." Kellan inserts them into his work from time to time. While the characters, almost always "extras," never look like him, all the significant markers that would be found in an actual self-portrait—the expressive elements, the smiles and frowns and brow tensions, etc....—have been transplanted from Kellan onto these characters' faces and into their body language[3a,3b].

^{3a} The origin of this "technique" extends back to when we were kids. Kellan would sometimes (maybe more than just sometimes) find it easier to draw characters that expressed how he was feeling than to explain how he was feeling to people who asked. As he got older, he got better at it until finally he spent a semester in art school creating a series of paintings that he referred to explicitly as self-portraits, each of which featured someone from his life carrying some of his inner matter in their expressions[3c]. I was one such person who was co-opted without permission into the project (he obtained permission from no one), which led to a minor argument between us that I'm not going to go

into here, other than to say that the painting made me queasy whenever I looked at it (and even in this moment, as I think about it, it makes me just as queasy).

[3b] The first use of this technique in his comics can be found in *I, Angel*, when the coat check girl at the country club that Amiel is invited to looks at herself in the mirror after handing Amiel a claim ticket for the fleece he leaves in her care.

[3c] I have reason to believe that aside from the project in college and in his work as a comic artist, Kellan might have done one more such self-portrait in his life, one in which he co-opted Natalie.

[4] It's really more like the perspective of something that is peeking out over the top of the ball as it rolls. The top third of the ball is visible in each panel, filling up the bottom half of the panel. The colored segments of the ball change to indicate the ball's motion. The golem is in the panel's top half, growing smaller and smaller. When the ball comes to rest, the size of the golem and the orientation of the ball's colors becomes fixed. The man appears and begins to grow larger until he fills the top half of the panel, at which point, portions of him begin to disappear until only his shins can be seen[4a].

[4a] This is all so hard to describe, and probably even harder to visualize. Maybe it's just easier to imagine Kellan trying to ride the ball to some escape from all of this, to imagine Kellan's consciousness trying to get away from these objects that hold the unpleasant weight of him, looking back at them as it flees.

[5] Because of a certain quality in the artwork[5a], I believe what is occurring in this sequence in the comic took Kellan by surprise; that the man's panic at the thought of the golem being dissolved by the water is really Kellan's panic at realizing that the golem cannot engage in one of Natalie's favorite activities[5b]. Whether he realized this before beginning this issue–if he knew before writing it that the golem needed to approach an ocean she could not enter–and wrote the issue out of that panic place or if he innocently waded into the issue–if he brought the golem all the way to the ocean's edge–before realizing what was going to happen, I'm unable to say.

[5a] a subtle instability in the lines that suggests a real-time struggle with something; a hard to describe instability that only registers in the deeper, unseeing tissues of the eyes as one is reading it.

[5b] Natalie loved to swim. She swam laps for exercise in a local pool on a regular basis and, during the beach season, went to the beach almost every day in the early morning to swim in the ocean before the swarms. She even taught Kellan, who, unsurprisingly, refused to learn as a child.

[6] Based on the sequence, I don't believe that this blank panel is blank like the ones I was hypothesizing about earlier (Issue 11, note 10 and Issue 12, note 5).

Issue 15

Cover: Same as previous, but here the golem's hand is crumbling in the other hand.

Summary:

The golem sits atop the man's shoulders as he walks down a busy commercial street, past restaurants and clothing stores. As they walk, the man grows taller; he stretches upward without any proportionate increase in his width. The golem is thrust to higher elevation by his growth. She looks to her left, through an apartment window on the third floor of a building, and sees a woman cooking at a stove. She then looks through a window on the next floor up and sees two children watching television. Through another window, one more floor up: a man reading a book. And on the next floor up: a goldfish in a bowl[1]. And the next: a man crushing a beer can against his forehead. And the next: a woman wearing a shower cap and a towel.

And then the roof, home to an entire flock of pigeons. Upon her arrival, the pigeons take flight in chaotic unison, flying a circular route around the golem and the man. They exit the circle (and then the panel) at the 270-degree point.

The man continues to grow, pushing the golem further skyward. She looks down and sees the cityscape below[2]: a series of intersecting freeways delineate a central space shaped like a human heart[3], 60% of the city within that space; roadways filled with red cars flow outward from the right side of it, roadways filled with blue cars flow inward toward it from the left. As the golem's distance from the ground increases, the city elements–buildings, houses, trees, and so forth–meld together into a yellow-brownish blur. Eventually, what the golem sees resembles a human-heart shape drawn by a finger in sand.

Suddenly, darkness settles onto the upper left portion of the heart. The golem looks up and sees an enormous cloud above: the cloud looks like a brain, suspended in the air. The golem soars toward the cloud, enters its interior, and finally, her head breaches its top surface. She looks up from there and sees the sun and a sliver of the moon about an inch to the sun's left[4].

A return to ordinary perspective: The man and the golem enter a candy store, walking side by side. The golem browses the candies and decides on black licorice. "Are you sure?" says the man. The golem nods. The man pays for the licorice. Side by side, the man and the golem exit the store[5].

The man and the golem enter a candy store, walking side by side. The golem browses the candies and decides on black licorice. "Are you sure?" says the man. The golem nods. The man pays for the black licorice. Side by side, the man and the golem exit the store.

The man and the golem enter a candy store, walking side by side. The golem browses the candies and decides on black licorice. "Are you sure?" says the man. The golem nods. The man pays for the black licorice. Side by side, the man and the golem exit the store.

The man and the golem enter a candy store, walking side by side. The golem browses the candies and decides on black licorice. "Are you sure?" says the man. The golem nods. The man pays for the black licorice. Side by side, the man and the golem exit the store.

The man and the golem enter a candy store, walking side by side. The golem browses the candies and decides on black licorice. "Are you sure?" says the man. The golem nods. The man pays for the licorice. Side by side, the man and the golem exit the store[6].

The man carries the golem up the pathway to the front door of his house. He unlocks the door, and they enter.

The man sits at the desk in his study, writing. He puts down his pen, picks up the pages, and stands. He journeys through the house: kitchen, stairwell, hallway, golem's bedroom[7].

The golem is in her bed, under the covers. The man sits in the captain's chair, reading to her from the pages that he holds. "1 awoke in his cell[8]," says the man, "and found a book he had never seen before lying on the table. He opened the book and began to read, and this is what he read: *When primitive humans developed language, there came a time to name the things of the body. And the first thing named was the hands and the last thing named was the heart. In between: the thumbs, the thighs, the elbows, the ears, the eyes, the teeth, the nostrils, the hair, the skin, the knees, the gut, the liver, the knuckles, the shins. And when all the things had been named, it was known that the body was finite.*" The golem interrupts. "Daddy," she says, "what's 'finite'?" "It means limited," says the man. "Like how you always eat all the Marshmallow Ka-Pows in the box. Every box of Marshmallow Ka-Pows is finite. It contains only a certain amount of cereal and no more than that. Got it?" The golem nods. The man continues reading. "*And so there came a time to name the infinite things.*" The man stops and looks at the golem. "Infinite," he says, "is kind of like the opposite of finite. It means limitless. Imagine a box of Marshmallow Ka-Pows that never runs out of cereal no matter how much you eat. That box would be infinite. Do you understand?" The golem puts a finger to her lips contemplatively. "Daddy," she says, "how big would the box be?" A thought bubble appears over the man's head containing a coffin. "Really big," he says. "Bigger than you?" she says. "Bigger than me," he says. "Wow," she says, "that is really big." "Are you ready to continue?" the man says. The golem nods. The man continues: "*And the first thing named was love and the last thing named was the soul.* 1 stopped reading and put down the book. He held up his left hand, held it directly in front of his face. With his right hand, he counted his fingers. When he was done, he counted something *on* his fingers. When he was done with that, he counted his fingers again. Then he used his left hand to count the fingers on his right hand. He looked puzzled. Then enlightened. The soul, he thought to himself, must be the capacity of something with only ten fingers to imagine something infinite."

The golem yawns loudly (speech bubble filled with YAWN). "Daddy," says the golem. "This is a good story, but I think I'm tired." "Ok," says the man. He folds the paper he holds, stands, and kisses the golem on the forehead. "Goodnight," he says. "Daddy?" says the golem. "Yes?" says the man. "I've been thinking," says the golem.

"About what?" says the man. "I know what I want to be for Halloween," says the golem. "And what's that?" says the man. "I want to be Window Eyes," says the golem. "Can I be Window Eyes for Halloween, Daddy?" The man scratches his head. "Uh, yeah," he says. "I guess. I mean, sure. Of course." "Thanks, Daddy," says the golem. "You can go now so I can sleep, ok?" The golem rolls over in the bed and pulls the covers up over herself. "Goodnight," the man says. "Goodnight," says the golem. The man walks to the door. He pauses in the doorway. He scratches his head. He turns off the lights.

Notes

---

[1] The goldfish is the only living thing she sees in these apartments that also notices her. It stares at her through the curved glass of its bowl.

[2] *Window Eyes* contains an abundance of aerial perspectives, particularly in the section featuring the child golem (something I am noticing more now that I am recounting than I had during the original read). The only other series in which Kellan employs aerial views to such a degree is *I, Angel.* Jeremy Stronk, in his criticism of that series, suggests that these perspectives are intended to evoke the sense that something above is watching everything take place (Kellan has refused to comment on whether this is true or not). It's possible that Kellan is doing something similar here. My friend never spoke of a belief in heaven, but even if he did not believe in it, he loved Natalie enough to create such a belief solely so he could imagine her there.

[3] Again, no resemblance to a lemon.

[4] While this sequence has the quality of a dream, nothing indicates that it is one[4a].

[4a] Sequences like this are found throughout Kellan's work (the underground flying sequence in *The Mall Beasts*, for instance), and it always infuriates Kellan when they are interpreted as dream. He doesn't understand why people need to believe that there is only dream and reality with no intervening states. "Life is impossible to understand when everything has to be one or the other," he once told me. "What is a feeling, for instance? Is that dream or is it reality? What is an orgasm? What is death? What is a vacation?"

[5] This sequence takes up exactly one page of parchment.

[6] While they were dating, Natalie introduced Kellan to the art of Sizemore Wallace. Kellan became enamored with a series of Wallace's called *The Abduction of Time*[6a]. The series consists of eight paintings, numbered one through eight, each of them identical, in all of which a man is shaving his face in front of a mirror. According to Wallace, each painting was painted from scratch, from his mind's eye, without the use of any copying mechanism or key, without reference to any of the paintings that came before, and captures a completely different

moment in the life of the man (in an interview, Wallace stated that the purpose of the series was to capture how life on the material plane is a series of echoes that only gains substance through the intervention of the intellectual and superconscious planes).

[6a] For Kellan's thirty-third birthday, Natalie painted him a series of paintings that she called "The Conduction of Time," five identical paintings, in all of which Kellan sits at his desk, a pen in his hand descending toward a blank sheet of paper.

[7] For the first time, a sense of how the house is laid out, though it is limited: Kellan allows us only a series of spatial relationships that unite the study with the golem's bedroom. It remains impossible to understand where anything else in the house exists in relation to this pathway (or to determine if the pathway presented is even the complete pathway between those two points in the house and not just glimpses of some parts of the complete version).

[8] This is a new scene from the universe of *The Digit*.

Issue 16[1]

Cover: Same as previous, but here the rest of the golem visible from the bottom of the hole crumbles.

Summary:

The man sits at his desk in the study. He is examining a small pair of glasses. On the desk, to the left of him: a box of toothpicks and a container of glue. The golem is not in the study with him[2], but she can be heard speaking from somewhere else in the house (her speech bubbles are in the study with the man). "Daddy," she says, "remember when Glassman upperhanded The Prime Slime and made him admit that he tried to poison all of Glassman's fish but he didn't know where Window Eyes is?" "I think you mean 'apprehended,'" says the man, "though I suppose that 'upperhanded' could be correct too." "Yes, apperhended him," says the golem, "and no matter what Glassman said to him, The Prime Slime still didn't know where Window Eyes is. Do you remember that?" The man puts the glasses down on the desk, selects a toothpick from the box and picks up the glue. He carefully lays the toothpick vertically on the right lens of the glasses. "Yes," he says. "I remember." "And do you remember when Glassman found the booprints for that spooky place and he went there and he looked for Window Eyes but all he found was spiderwebs and old dolls?" says the golem. "Blueprints," says the man as he glues the toothpick to the center of the lens. "He found blueprints, not booprints." "Right," says the golem.

The man picks up another toothpick, lays it on the left lens. "Daddy," says the golem, "do you remember when Glassman ate dinner all by himself in the diner and the waitress came over and asked him where is Window Eyes and Glassman knocked over his cup of water because he was per-pless?" "Perplexed," says the man, as he glues the toothpick up the center of the left lens. "Right," says the golem, "he was so perplecked that he didn't even know not to knock over his water. Remember?" "Yes," says the man. "I remember." The man takes out another toothpick and snaps it in half. He lays one of the pieces on the right side of the stick glued to the right lens, at the lens' horizontal center, perpendicular to the glued stick, and the other piece on the left side in the same fashion; glues them into place. "Daddy," says the golem. "Do you remember when Glassman found the scarf that belonged to Window Eyes in the lost and found at the lie-berry and he thought it was a clue and he searched the whole entire lie-berry but he couldn't find anything and then the lie-berry Anne told him that the scarf had been there for a whole year and so Glassman knew that it wasn't really a clue, just something that made him sad?" Viewed from behind, the man picks up the glasses and holds them before his eyes, glued-side away, so that he can look through the lenses in the same direction as someone wearing the glasses would look through them. Then the view shifts to in front of him, and the man is seen *through* the four toothpick-delineated quadrants of the right lens, his image slightly refracted. The view shifts back: he puts the glasses down on the desk, picks up another toothpick and snaps it in half. He begins to glue the halves to the left lens in the same way that he glued halves to the right lens. "Daddy?" says the golem. "Yes?" says the man. "Do you remember?" says the golem. "Remember what?" says the man. "What I just said," says the golem. "Do you remember about Glassman and the lie-berry?" "Right," says the man. "Yes. I remember, yes."

The man and the golem are in the golem's bedroom. The man is kneeling, helping the golem get her left arm into a long-sleeve, pink body suit. "Are you sure there's no tutu?" says the golem. "I'm sure," says the man. "But I really think there's supposed to be a tutu," says the golem. "We don't have a tutu," says the man, "so there isn't a tutu." "Ok," says the golem, as her arm slides into the bodysuit. "Daddy?" she says. "Yes?" says the man. "Do you remember when Glassman had that doll he took from that room in the spooky house and he was on the floor of the headquarters and he started talking to it and I said why is he talking to a doll and you said because he has no other choice?" "Yes," says the man, picking the glasses from earlier off the floor. "I remember." The man opens the arms of the glasses. He slides the glasses on to the golem's face. He adjusts how the glasses sit on the golem's face. The next panel features a portrait-style view of the golem wearing the glasses[3]: in addition to the toothpicks seen previously, the man has glued popsicle sticks in a rectangle around each lens so that each of the lenses now looks like a small window frame. The galaxy mark on her cheek is visible through the frame that's closest to the right side of the panel. Then a return to the view of the man and the golem in the room. "Daddy?" says the golem. "Yes?" says the man. "How do I look?" says the golem. The man stands up to take in the view. He looks at the golem. He cocks his head to the right, considering her from a second angle. He straightens his neck. He opens his mouth to speak, produces an empty speech bubble. Then he starts to cry.

Visible at a distance, the man and the costumed golem, who holds a molded-plastic pumpkin Halloween basket, walk on a suburban neighborhood sidewalk. If the panel is a lens we are looking through, they are facing it head-on. Over the course of five or so panels, they move up the sidewalk toward the reader. The golem, in these panels, is captured in some aspect of a skip, her basket captured in some aspect of a sway. By the fourth panel, they are close enough that it's possible to see that the man is still crying. By the fifth, the only part of the golem visible is her head; the panel is mostly about the man (from the mid-torso up) and his tears.

The man and the golem turn up a walkway in someone's front yard. They approach the door. The door opens. "Happy Halloween," says the woman standing in the open doorway in a witch costume. The woman holds a basket of candy out for the golem. As the golem searches through it, the woman turns her head to the man and sees that he is crying. She quickly turns back to the golem and then looks at the man out of the corner of her eyes. Then away, then out of the corner again. "I'll take this one," says the golem, holding up a small candy bar. "Thank you." "Happy Halloween," says the woman, her head still turned toward the golem, her eyes on the man. She retreats back into her house and closes the door.

The man and the golem on the sidewalk again. They turn up another walkway, knock on the door. A man, dressed as a werewolf, answers. "Happy Halloween," says the werewolf. "Happy Halloween!" says the golem. "And what are you supposed to be?" says the werewolf, holding out a bowl filled with candy. "I'm Window Eyes," says the golem. The werewolf looks confused. "I'm sorry," he says, "I don't know that one." "You don't know Window Eyes?" says the golem, the shape of her eyes and her mouth distended to express the disbelief she is experiencing. "No," says the werewolf, "I don't. I'm sorry." The werewolf then notices the man is crying. Like the woman at the other house, the werewolf quickly turns away. He tries to keep his attention on the golem as the golem selects a piece of candy from the bowl.

The man and the golem on the sidewalk again. Another walkway, another knock. A woman in an army uniform answers the door, says "Happy Halloween," holds out a bowl of candy, notices immediately that the man is crying. "I'm sorry," she says to the man. "Are you ok?" The man doesn't answer. The woman turns to look at the golem. "Is your father ok?" says the woman. Then her face contorts to indicate shock. "My daddy is broken right now," says the golem. Close-up of the golem's face[4]: some of the man's tears have fallen on the top of her head and have run down across her forehead and cheeks, softening the clay, carving tiny river basins into the golem's skin. Return to the full scene: man, woman, golem. "Don't worry," says the golem. "He'll be better soon." The woman doesn't know what to do or where to look. She continues to hold out the bowl, to hold back as much of what she is feeling as possible while the golem selects some candy.

The man and the golem walk up the walkway to the man's house. The man is still crying.

The man and the golem on the stairs, the basket in the golem's hand. The man is still crying.

The man and golem in the man's bedroom. The man is still crying. The golem puts the basket down on the floor and helps the man, still fully clothed, into bed. The golem pulls the covers over the man. "Don't worry, Daddy," says the golem. "Everything is going to be ok." She kisses him on the forehead. Then she sits on the floor next to the basket and begins eating candy from it.

Notes

---

[1] I had a dream last night that I was Kellan, reading and editing these summaries. I/He seemed to be particularly concerned about the portrayal of himself in the footnotes and was constantly making the same correction over and over, replacing the name Kellan with the name Thomas. Afterwards, I (as myself, I think, though I may still have been Kellan) called Egret and told her that something was wrong with the manuscript. She asked me what it was and I told her I didn't know anyone named Thomas. She said she was coming over to look at the manuscript, but when she arrived, she only looked at me. Finally, she took a pen out of her pocket and wrote the word Kellan on my forehead. I tried to stop her, but I was too weak. End of dream.

[2] I suppose the golem could be in the study but hidden in some corner that we are not permitted to see.

[3] The word "portrait" might call to mind something far more formal than what was found here, so to clarify: it was like Kellan captured the golem in a moment during which she naturally, through happenstance, resembled someone posing for a portrait.

[4] Similar in execution to the close-up that occurred after the man put the glasses on her.

Issue 17[1]

Cover: Once again from the bottom of the hole, looking up to see the moon, unobstructed, in the sky.

Summary:

The man is in his kitchen, holding a telephone to his ear[2], talking to someone unidentified. "She won't take it off," he says. "She refuses to wear anything else. She won't even talk to me unless I let her wear it." He paces toward the refrigerator. "You don't think I've tried that?" He opens the door. "No, not worried. Worried isn't the right word." He looks inside the fridge. "I just don't know what to do. Should I be worried?" He closes the door. "I'm not going to 'discipline' her." He opens the door again. The view shifts to the contents of the refrigerator: A carton of eggs (on the top shelf), a jar of mayonnaise[3] (middle shelf), an onion (bottom shelf)[4]. The view shifts back to the man: He slaps his neck and pulls his hand away. Close-up on his open hand: a black smear that once was a mosquito[5] (tiny insectile bits are visible at the edges of the smear: a leg, a proboscis), across the center of which is a bold red stripe[6]. "I'm not going to do that either." He wipes his hand on his pants. He reaches into the fridge and pulls out the mayonnaise jar with his free hand. "I think I just wanted to talk to someone about this so that it would seem more familiar to me. I guess I thought hearing myself say the things that I've been thinking about would make them more familiar." He turns from the fridge and begins to walk across the kitchen. "She's quieter, doesn't ask as many questions. Maybe she's just growing up." The jar, for no available reason, slips from the man's hand. The perspective follows the falling jar as it passes the man's waist, his knees, his shins: a final glimpse of it intact at the moment of contact with the floor[7].

Notes

[1] There were two issues numbered 17. The first, presented here, was incomplete. It seemed that Kellan had started down a path with this issue and then changed his mind and went in a different direction, but instead of disposing of the unfinished draft, he decided to include it.

[2] The phone is an older phone from the 1980s. It is connected to a landline and has a spiraling cord that connects the quarter-moon shaped receiver to the phone's base[2a].

[2a] Even given the absence of time signifiers, this item is out of sync temporally with the rest of the comic[2b].

[2b] But it is not the first time that such a phone has appeared in Kellan's work. The trio in *Crusteacean Wedding* use phones like this for phone sex escapades because they feel like "fucking shouldn't ever be digital," and Darby refuses to use any other type of phone in *Cupcakes* because he finds the extra weight of the receiver (as compared to the weight of a cell phone) to be comforting.

[3] Munduson's wholesale brand, the same mayonnaise that Amiel favors in *I, Angel*, and also the mayonnaise in *Tramplemundus* that Typhoon Wednesday Maniac throws into the eyes of Polygon Two during the televised battle that viewers of the news program it was featured on mistook as a scene from a new game show.

[4] The focus here is on the absence of foodstuffs, the fallow fields of the empty refrigerator. It is both a symbol of emotional famine and also a direct reference to Natalie, who quite literally came into Kellan's life and filled his refrigerator with food. Before her, his refrigerator was always empty, save for a few onions (Kellan, for all his particularity about food, used to eat onions like they were apples) and various condiments. He subsisted mostly on cereal, foods that you rehydrate–noodle packets and the like–and large amounts of freeze-dried ice cream (which he did not rehydrate) that he ordered by the case from an outdoor sporting good supplier.

[5] Yes, it would be unusual for someone to encounter a mosquito in what must be at least November[5a], but at this point, there's every indication

that feeling has subsumed causality in Kellan's mind; or, as Kellan would have put it, that symbol has reclaimed reality from fact[5b].

[5a] I presume here, based on the changing of seasons during the walk montages in the earlier issues, that the man lives in a place where it is cool or even cold in the months after Halloween.

[5b] The actual quote of his that I am drawing on comes from, of all places, *Harpoon Follies,* from the scene in which Ahab declares his devotion to Mobitha. "Our love shall be its own ocean," he says, "and through it, symbol shall reclaim reality from fact."

[6] I think the red was actual blood. It sat on the page unevenly, like a crust that had formed over the black ink[6a].

[6a] Whether the blood was his or came from an animal, I don't know.

[7] This is the last panel of the issue (the remainder of the issue's 32 pages from this point forward are blank). The jar never breaks. The image is like the one of the egg in Issue 5, capturing a normally imperceptible moment: the moment when a fragile object first makes contact with the floor[7a]. We generally only see such an object when it is whole *or* when it is in contact with the floor, but we are unable to perceive that unique moment when the object is both whole *and* in contact with the floor.

[7a] No doubt an allusion to the work of Angie Connell, another artist Kellan favors who once did a series of paintings called "Vulnerability" in which she captures a variety of collisions (fruit with wall, car with tree, ball with head, etc....) at the precise moment of initial contact, the delicate onset of the catastrophe. In the absence of the violence that exists in fluid time, she manages to infuse these moments with an eerie tenderness[7b].

[7b] Kellan's favorite of these paintings (much to my surprise) is of a bird flying into a window. In the painting, the tip of the bird's beak connects to the tip of its reflection in the glass, creating the illusion of a kiss. After Natalie found this out, she started calling Kellan "her little window bird," which he claimed to hate.

ISSUE 17

Cover: Once again from the bottom of the hole, looking up to see the moon in the sky[1].

Summary:

[The entire issue is presented as a photo album. Each of the silent panels is drawn to look like a photo that has been pasted to the page. The number of photos on a page varies from one to three[2].]

The golem, in her Window Eyes costume, sitting at a window that looks into the backyard[3], staring out that window. A tree visible in the yard is adorned with orange and red leaves.

The golem, in her Window Eyes costume, sitting at a window that looks into the backyard, staring out that window. A tree visible in the yard is adorned with yellow and brown leaves.

The golem, in her Window Eyes costume, sitting at a window that looks into the backyard, staring out that window. A tree visible in the yard is clinging to the remaining half of its leaves, all of which are yellow and brown.

The golem, in her Window Eyes costume, sitting at a window that looks into the backyard, staring out that window. A small number of brown leaves remain on the tree.

The golem, in her Window Eyes costume, sitting at a window that looks into the backyard, staring out that window. The tree is completely bare.

The golem, in her Window Eyes costume, sitting at a window that looks into the backyard, staring out that window. The tree branches hold snow.

A view of a piece of the landscape outside the window: mostly the sky, a cloud and a bird, snippets of the tree, some brown leaves[4].

A view of a piece of the landscape outside the window: branches holding snow, the cloudless sky beyond them.

A view of a piece of the landscape outside the window: fence bottom, grassy ground, several stick-markers, brown and yellow and orange leaves on the ground like litter.

What is supposed to be a blurry photograph of an obscure portion of the window area, including, in the bottom left corner, what seems to be a small section of the golem's head[5].

The man's hand, open, palm facing up, the remains of a mosquito in the center of it (black smear, insectile parts, bold red stripe[6]).

A view of a piece of the landscape outside the window: trunk of the tree, the fence behind it.

A view of a piece of the landscape outside the window: some sky, a portion of the fence that separates the yard from the yard adjacent to it, a yellow leaf sailing through the air.

[7]The man and the golem in a rose garden, standing in front of a bush that's pushing blushing orange roses into the world.

The man and the golem posing next to a plastic-mold statue of Moosipher inside a Munduson's.

The man and the golem, poking their heads through a carnival cutout, she through the face-hole of a strongman body, he through the face-hole of a dog[8].

The man and the golem at the dinner table, candidly looking up from their bowls of cereal and at the camera.

The man and the golem on a boat. The man looks distressed. His arm is wound tightly around the golem, who stands directly in front of him, wearing him like a second life-vest.

The man and the golem at a petting zoo, the golem with her arms wrapped around the neck of a goat, the man on one knee on the other side of the goat.

The man and the golem in front of a white background[9].

The man and the golem, location unknown, the man on one knee, the golem next to him, holding her arm up behind him, holding up two fingers on her hand behind his head to create "bunny ears."

The man and the golem, location unknown, pointing to and looking at the moon in the sky.

The man and the golem in an art museum, their backs to the camera, looking at a painting that hangs on the wall[10].

The man and the golem at a circus, at the front entrance of the circus's large red and white tent[11].

The man and the golem in a golf cart, location unknown, the golem in the driver's seat, looking through the plastic windshield, her right leg struggling to reach the accelerator, the man sitting next to her, looking at the camera.

The front of the man's house.

A birthday cake, "happy birthday" written in blue icing, thirty-something candles stuck into the cake.

The beach ball, sitting on a pea-soup colored carpeted floor.

The man standing in front of a mirror, shirtless, his stomach sucked in to make his ribs visible, the camera obscuring the part of his face that's centered at his left eye.

The beach ball, sitting in the opening of a bucket on the grass in a yard.

The grandfather clock, the man's reflection thinly visible in the glass face of the clock.

The golem, lying on a wooden table, naked[12].

A bowl of Ka-Pows, taken from above, a blushing orange rose propped up off the table, its top half resting on the edge of the bowl, the flower hanging over the cereal and milk.

There are no photos on the final page of the issue, only these words written in a highly stylized calligraphy:

"Human life is precious. Human endeavor is foolish. Grief is the reconciliation."
—The Overseer[13]

Notes

---

[1] I examined the covers of both the issues numbered 17. At the time, I felt certain that there was a difference that I was intuiting but could not locate. Now, I am less certain but more agitated. They seemed identical. They could have been otherwise.

[2] I cannot guarantee that I have remembered every photo. What is presented here is what is remembered.

[3] The small portion of the room she is in contains no visible clues as to which room it is; it is either a room never before seen or a never before seen section of a room we are familiar with.

[4] I believe that this sequence is supposed to capture the man's attempts to figure out, using the zoom function of the camera, what it is that the golem is looking for/at as she sits at the window.

[5] Based on what comes immediately after, my guess is that the man was bitten by a mosquito as he was taking this photo, causing him to jerk and capture something other than what was intended.

[6] This I also believe to be actual blood for the reasons previously stated.

[7] In the sequence of photos that begins here, time is elusive. Since the golem is not wearing the glasses in any of them, they were probably taken prior to Halloween, but beyond that it's impossible to say whether the meaning in their placement is a temporal one or if there is some atemporal logic at work.

[8] The astute reader might be wondering who it is that is taking these photos. The answer is we don't know. Yet another nebulous space that Kellan has crafted, like the layout of the house or the out-of-panel things that the man and clay woman point to during their strolls.[2a]

[8a] Jeremy Stronk once wrote: "Kellan is not frivolous with the space he creates. Every space in his work is carefully designed to hold something, even if that something is nothing.[8b]"

[8b] I suppose it's possible that's what's happening here, that Kellan built these spaces to hold a nothingness; that he wanted this work to contain a vast negative space that reflected an emptiness he was feeling. I wouldn't fault anyone for arriving at that conclusion. But, it doesn't

feel right to me. Natalie changed something in him that her death could not undo. If I had to describe it, I'd say that the post-Natalie Kellan no longer believes in that sort of emptiness[8c]. Being with Natalie taught him that what once appeared to him to be emptiness was something that he was shutting out because he thought it would overwhelm him. I offer, therefore, a different conclusion: this space is about him being open. It's meant to hold something that Kellan cannot express on his own because he's not big enough to contain it within himself; he has created the space as a bridge between the work and the imaginations of its readers, allowing the readers to provide the extra capacity to hold what Kellan alone cannot[8d].

[8c] which could be something he finally realized about himself while working on the refrigerator scene in the other issue 17, hence that issue being replaced as the official issue 17[8e].

[8d] "And what we cannot contain, we cannot express without sacrifice." – part of the code that constitutes the operating system of the robots in *A Conspiracy of Slumber*.

[8e] Although it is possible that the first issue 17 *is* the official one and the second version, though it seems complete where the other is not, is the extra.

[9] Or is this more blankness, an abduction of the world from the moment that it resided in.

[10] Silbana Il'Trusco's *The Flower Eaters*, which depicts a group of bankers in a garden, plucking flowers from the bushes with their mouths and eating them.

[11] This photo might be related to the photo with the strongman and dog cutouts, even though it was not presented in sequence with it.

[12] This photo is drawn to look like it's been crumpled and then crudely rescued from that crumpled state.

[13] Not from the published version of *The Digit*, in which the Overseer is an unseen presence never quoted directly.

Cover: Same as previous, but now a little girl is leaning over into the hole, peering down into it, the moon in the sky partially obscured by her.

Summary:

Front of the man's house: no one present in the yard or visible through the windows. A caption in the upper right corner of the panel: "And Seraphim said: 'The success of a nation should not be measured in the wealth of its richest citizens but in the wealth of its poorest.'[1]"

Interior of the house: the man sits at his desk, writing. Without looking up, he calls out to the golem. "Are you hungry?" he says. "I'm almost done here." The man continues writing for a few panels. He calls out to the golem again. "Are you hungry?" he says. The man continues writing for a panel. He stops and looks up. "Hello?" he says. "Where are you?" As he awaits her answer, the perspective moves to directly behind him, in line with his eyes. Beyond the back of his head, a window is visible, and beyond that, the sticks that have been stuck into the earth in the backyard are visible. The perspective remains fixed as the man's head turns and his profile comes into view[2]. A speech bubble leaks from his mouth: "Hello?" he says. "I'm talking to you." Full-room perspective: the man stands up from the desk and exits the study. He appears in the kitchen. "Hello?" he says. He appears in the living room: "Are we playing hide and seek?" he says. He opens a closet and looks inside, finding only the detritus of suburban life (a broom, extra blankets and pillows, cans of bug spray…). He appears in the doorway to one of the bathrooms. "I'm seeking you," he says. He appears in a room that has not been exhibited in any of the previous issues (it contains a stationary bike, an ottoman, and a vacuum). "Are you in here?" he says. He appears in the golem's bedroom. A caption reads: "In survivalism, cunning is the highest trait, but in post-survivalism, or what we might call enlightenmentism, the highest trait is compassion." He looks under her bed. He stands up. The small circles that connect a character's head to a thought bubble form to the right of his head, connecting to the next panel which is shaped like a thought bubble. That panel depicts a pile of dirt on the floor of an unspecified room, a small galaxy mark visible in its surface.

A frantic search takes place:

The man in the backyard, near a tree, the distress on his face at Level 1[3]. A thought bubble from his head is overlaid on the yard so that the upper part of what's visible of the tree, part of the fence, and some of the ground in this panel are outside the bubble while the lower part of the tree, part of the fence and some of the ground are inside it. Entirely inside the thought bubble: the golem, translucent, sits at the base of the tree, running her hands through the grass[4].

The man in the kitchen again, the distress on his face at Level 2. Another overlaid thought bubble: the golem, translucent, sitting at the kitchen table, eating a bowl of cereal[5,6].

The man in the study, the distress on his face at Level 3. Another overlaid thought bubble: the golem, her hand on one of the drawers in the man's desk, about to open it. This golem, still translucent, appears slightly larger than the previous golem.

The man in the golem's bedroom again, the distress on his face at Level 4. Overlaid thought bubble: the golem, lying in bed, looking toward the captain's chair like she's listening to the man read her a story. This golem appears slightly larger and more translucent than the previous golem (the lines and colors of which she consists are slightly lighter).

The man in the living room, the distress on his face at Level 5. Overlaid thought bubble: the golem, looking at the television, leaning slightly to the left as if she's resting on someone else's shoulder. This golem appears slightly larger and more translucent than the previous golem (the lines and colors of which she consists have grown slightly lighter still[7]). Small breasts have appeared on her chest[8].

The man in another new room (this room contains: a love seat, a shoe rack, and an unopened patio umbrella), the distress on his face at Level 6. Overlaid thought bubble: the golem, sitting on the floor, drawing with crayons on a sheet of paper. This golem is the size of a grown woman and more translucent than the previous golem (lines and colors continuing to grow lighter). She continues to have breasts.

The man in the dining room, the distress on his face at Level 7. Overlaid thought bubble: the golem sitting at one end of the dining table, eating a bowl of cereal. This golem is the same size as the previous golem and more translucent (lines and colors lighter). It has also begun to lose detail. It maintains a female body shape and the galaxy on its cheek but has moved slightly along the spectrum from 'clay person' toward 'mound of mud with unusually distinct humanoid features.'

The man in another new room (the room contains a coat rack, an inflatable alligator-shaped pool raft, and a pair of large stereo speakers)[9], the distress on his face at Level 8. Overlaid thought bubble: the golem sitting on the floor, playing with a doll. This golem is the same size as the previous golem, more translucent (lighter lines, colors, etc.) and now, though still suffering from a loss of definition, looks more like one of the failed adult golems than it does like the young girl golem.

The man in the living room, the distress on his face at Level 9. Overlaid thought bubble: the golem sitting on the couch, wearing the Window Eyes glasses[10], looking through a photo album. This golem is one of the failed adult golems and is more translucent (even lighter, etc.) than the previous golem.

The man in the golem's bedroom, his face annihilated. Overlaid thought bubble: the golem (adult) lying on the bed seductively, looking at the captain's chair like she's listening to someone read to her. This golem is almost entirely translucent, a ghost.

The man, his face still a wreck, races out the front door of his house and up the pathway that leads to the sidewalk. He stops at the sidewalk. He turns his head left. Caption: "Capitalism inherently favors the sociopath who is unencumbered by concerns for other people." Then he looks right. His eyes open wide. The man rushes to the right. He comes to the place where the bus dropped the golem off in Issue 12. The golem, sans glasses, sits on the curb. Next to her, a small rolling suitcase. The man's face regenerates its normal composition. He sits down next to her. "What are you doing?" says the man. "It's not a school day." "I'm not going to school," says the golem. "Then what?" says the man. "I'm going to go look for Window Eyes." "I see," says the man. "What's your plan?" "I can't fly and I can't swim," says the golem, "so I have to take the bus." "I don't think this bus goes to Shaidun," says the man. "I don't know what else to do," says the golem. "I have to go find her." The golem starts to cry. Milky streams of animal fat run down her cheeks. "I have to go," she says again. The man stands and picks her up off the curb. He holds her aloft in a hug as she cries. He picks up the small suitcase and walks back toward the house.

The golem is in the bed in the man's bedroom, under the covers. The man enters the room and sits on the bed next to her. He kisses her on the forehead. "How are you feeling?" he says. "Sleepy," says the golem. "You've had a long day," says the man. "I have," says the golem. "Can I sleep in here tonight?" "Yes," says the man. He leans forward and kisses her on the forehead again. He backs away and stands up from the bed. He turns from the golem. "Daddy?" says the golem. "Is Glassman ever going to find Window Eyes?" The man turns back. "I don't know," he says. "I wish you knew," says the golem. "Me too," says the man. The golem yawns. "Goodnight, Daddy," says the golem. "Goodnight," says the man. The golem turns on her side and closes her eyes. The man adjusts the blanket to better cover her. As he is doing this, he looks up. His eyes go wide. A caption in a blue box over his head: "And Seraphim said: Love motivates us to build a world that is far, far different from the world that death has led us to." The perspective shifts so that what the man is looking at is visible: the head of an enormous earthworm peers through a window into the bedroom.

Notes

[1] This quote and the ones that come later in this issue[1a] do not seem to correlate to what is happening around them. I can think of only two reasons for why they are here: 1. Kellan is challenging how the reader expects art to work[1b] (and so these quotes have nothing to do with what's going on precisely *because* the reader is anticipated to expect them to). 2. Kellan tends to become grandiose in response to challenging emotions[1c] (and so these quotes are really indirect expressions of annihilating emotions that Kellan is trying to manage, emotions that do in fact pertain to the events depicted[1d]).

[1a] which do not come from any published version of *Maze on Dixon* and are therefore likely from a "story" that the man is writing for the golem, perhaps the story he is writing when we encounter him at the beginning of this issue.

[1b] One of Kellan's primary goals as an artist is to encourage the deconditioning of the imagination, which he sees as being habituated over time by education and social pressures. It is therefore common for him to do things in his work that seem unexplainable to anyone who expects the work to conform to the standards that have been set by previous works, things that maybe are unexplainable but nonetheless possess meaning and value if their existence is appreciated without judgment[1e].

[1c] This is not to say that the things Kellan says at those times do not carry weight, but those who know him can always sense that beyond what is being said, no matter what its magnitude, there always lurks an emotion, an awfully personal emotion.

[1d] It might help to think of Kellan as having split, his intellectual self from his emotional self, each of them suddenly operating independent of the other.

[1e] Miranda Yarba, another of his critics, has written about this better than I ever could in "The Clocks of Cupcakes," her analysis of the abundance of time pieces found in *Cupcakes* (she counts close to one hundred and fifty clocks, watches, and sundials in the series's twenty-

four issues) and the impossible timelines they create if the times they display are assumed to be accurate.

[2] He is rendered here in such a way as that his head, which up till this point has always appeared three dimensional, appears two dimensional. It is a perfect profile missing all the elements that give depth to his face.

[3] Instead of describing what the face looks like, I'm going to allow the reader to see the distress however they see it and escalate it as they wish. That makes the experience more personal, which is in line with what Kellan was, in my estimation, attempting to do here with the art.

[4] The continuity between what is inside the bubbles and outside the bubbles in this panel is seamless, the difference being primarily in the coloration: the golem is exclusively translucent; the inside-the-bubble parts of the objects that straddle the in and the out (such as the tree or the fence or ground in this first panel) appear as if a translucent version of those parts has been laid over a solid version. In other words, it seems as if Kellan inked and colored a scene in which the man stands entirely by himself in the backyard near the tree and then, after that was done, he added the thought bubble, rendering the golem with that translucent quality *plus* adding, with that same translucent quality, a new version of everything in the thought bubble that was already in the pre-thought bubble version of the panel (the bottom of the tree, a lower part of the fence, some of the ground in the vicinity of the golem), drawing these new versions directly on top of the old.

[5] In lieu of clumsily attempting to describe this effect over and over, just know that each of these panels with overlaid thought bubbles is rendered in the same style as the first, with the thought bubble being seamlessly overlaid onto the scene to create the impression that the man, as he searches, is either remembering or imagining a version of the golem-less space in which the golem is present.

[6] The accessories that the golem is using in some of these scenes (the bowl of cereal, etc.) are also translucent.

[7] It should be noted that of the things rendered translucent, it is my presumption that only the golem is fading. The objects that appear twice (once in the solid world the man inhabits and once in the imaginary or remembered world overlaid on the solid world) are

difficult to assess, but I see no reason why Kellan would have portrayed their stability as decaying, especially given that the accessories, which are readily available to us, maintain a consistent level of presence that contrasts jarringly with what is happening to the golem.

[8] The transformation of the golem in this sequence is difficult to describe. The golem does not seem to be aging, only morphing into something else. Nor is there a sexualization of the golem. The changes that bring her closer to womanhood appear awkward and grotesque, conveying the man's distress and nothing else.

[9] Based on what happens in this sequence, I have come to believe that these are rooms that the man and the woman he lost never had the chance to convert into specific spaces while she was alive. They sit perpetually in these seemingly random states. I further conject that the child golem's bedroom was once one of these rooms.

[10] This is the only golem in this sequence wearing the glasses.

ISSUE 19

Cover: Similar to previous, but here the girl is climbing down into the hole.

Summary:

The man races through the house with the golem in his arms[1], surrounded by a horrible screeching sound (the word "SCREECH" is written across the panels, the number of "E"s increased significantly to extend the length of the word; the black letters bleed across the void space between the panels so that the word is never interrupted by that space, snake down and back through the panels when they reach either edge of the page so that the word remains continuous throughout the sequence–sometimes flowing with the left-to-right-direction of the read and sometimes flowing against it–and are always backgrounded relative to the man and the golem, disappearing behind them any time they intersect in the two-dimensional landscape of the comic). "Daddy," says the golem, as they race through the living room, "what are those things?" "They're called Legions," says the man. "They're supposed to hold the Earth together." "Why?" says the golem. "That's their job," says the man. "Why are they here?" says the golem. "They're here for you," says the man. "Are they mad at me?" says the golem. "No," says the man. "They're mad at *me*." "What did you do?" says the golem.

The man and golem enter the man's study[2]. The screeching does not follow them, but two giant earthworms are visible in the backyard through the study's windows. The worms are large enough that only a portion of their bodies can be visible at any given moment[3]. One of them peers into the house. The other has its head buried in the ground where the failed adult golems rest. For several panels, the man and golem remain locked in a "stare" with the peering worm. During those panels, the other worm seems to be eating the remains of the adult golems. It pulls its head out of the earth, appears to chew, sticks it head back in the earth, pulls it out, appears to chew. Then the peering worm opens its maw and emits a new screech. The golem screams. "It's ok," the man says. "It's going to be ok." "Can they come and get us?" says the golem. "I don't know," says the man. "What are we going to do?" says the golem. "We need to drive them away," says the man. "Can't we just ask them to leave?" says the golem. "It doesn't work that way," says the man. "We need to go to the kitchen."

The man and the golem enter the kitchen. He is no longer carrying her, but he holds her hand as she stands by his side. He leads her to a pantry closet. He opens it. A panel from the perspective of someone looking into the closet:

The items on the closet's three shelves are immaculately organized, though many of them are generic[4]. The top shelf contains canned goods labeled corn, beans, beets, crushed tomatoes, etc.… The bottom shelf contains boxed goods labeled pasta, flour, brown sugar, etc.… The middle shelf contains condiments in an array of containers, small jars of cinnamon and thyme, a large jar filled with dried chili peppers, a cardboard cylinder labeled salt…

The man takes the cylinder marked salt from the closet. "Stay here," says the man. "Stay under the table." "I don't have my Window Eyes glasses," says the golem. "What?" says the man. He opens a small metallic spout on the top of the cylinder. "My Window Eyes glasses," says the golem, "I don't have them. I packed them so no one would know who I was until I wanted them to." "We can get them later," says the man. He pours a small pile of salt into his hand. "But I need them now," says the golem. "They can keep me safe." "We don't have time," says the man. He licks the top of the salt pile. "I need them," screams the golem. Another screech rattles through the house[5]. The man looks at the golem and then out the kitchen window where a section of the body of one of the worms can be seen. "Stay here," he says, pouring the salt from his hand back into the container. "I'll be right back."

The man races through the house[6], from the kitchen to the golem's bedroom. He kneels next to the suitcase the golem had with her in the last issue, puts the still open container of salt on the floor. He rifles through the suitcase, retrieving the glasses. He accidentally knocks the salt container over and spills some salt on the floor. "Shit," he says. He quickly tries to gather as much of the salt as he can into his hands. He stands up. He races.

The man returns to the kitchen. The golem is under the table. He hands her the glasses. "Stay here," he says.

Blank panel.

Blank panel.

Blank panel[7].

The man outside in the moonlit backyard, container of salt in his hand, the two worms looming above him, looking down on him[8]. "Leave us alone," says the man[9]. One of the worms spits a torrent of dirt down on the man[10]. The man shields himself with his arms. The torrent stops. "Leave now," he says[11]. The other worm dives at him. The man leaps to the side as the worm snaps its maw closed where the man had been. The man quickly empties salt into his hand from the container[12]. He hurls it at the worm that just attacked him. The worm screeches and flails wildly. The spitter worm dives at the man. The man dodges. He reloads his hand with salt and hurls it. The spitter worm screeches and flails. The man continues his attack, hurling salt at both the worms. They screech, they flail, the spitter vomits dirt into the sky. Eventually, they dive into the earth and disappear. The man looks around the yard. The ground is torn up and littered with some of the sticks that had marked the burial sites.

The golem sits under the table in the kitchen, wearing the glasses. She looks more curious than scared. The man appears in the kitchen doorway. "Are you ok?" he says. "Yes," says the golem. "Is it safe now?" "I drove them away," says the man. "You can come out." The golem emerges from beneath the table. She runs to the man and wraps her arms around his waist. "Are they going to come back?" says the golem, looking up at the man as she hugs him. "I think so," says the man. "Probably. Yes." "What are we going to do?" says the golem. "I'll figure something out," says the man. "Daddy?" says the golem. "Yes?" says the man. "Could the Lesions have taken Window Eyes?" says the golem. The man doesn't answer. He picks the golem up into his arms. "Let's get you into bed," says the man. "But what if they come back?" says the golem. "They won't come back tonight," says the man. "Promise?" says the golem. "Promise," says the man.

The man carries the golem to his bedroom and puts her into bed. He kisses her goodnight.

The man in his study, writing something on a piece of paper.

The man in the backyard with a shovel in his hand. He crosses the yard to one of the holes created by the worms' escape into the earth. He looks up at the moon. He dives into the hole.

Return to the empty study, view from above the desk looking down on it, a piece of paper sitting on top. Zoom in once: it is clear now that there are words written on the page, though the words are unreadable. Zoom a second time, into the final panel: the words are now visible: "Went to find Window Eyes. Back soon. -Dad"

Notes

---

[1] The panels leap from room to room, but not in a way that betrays the obfuscation of the house's layout.

[2] It's unclear whether the man answers the golem's question. He certainly doesn't do it in view of the reader, but time had to have passed as they traversed from the living room to wherever in the house the study is, so it is possible that he does answer her in the transition.

[3] Based on my recollections, I estimate them to have the girth of the average birch trees where we grew up in Indiana. They might be as long as a quarter of a football field.

[4] I don't believe this is convenience. As I've said earlier, Kellan feels the small details are important. For him to make these items generic has to be a large gesture; in their genericness, they possess more significance than carefully elucidated items.

[5] Possibly in response to the golem's scream.

[6] Every sequence of panels in which the man is moving from one point in the house to another is different[6a].

[6a] I'm not sure I remember all the routes portrayed (or the parts of the routes portrayed) accurately[6b], but I did, around this point in my reading, return to other issues, ones in which the man moves through the house, so I could compare the routes and remember absolutely that each of them was unique, which is illogical, either on the part of the man, who sometimes took unnecessarily complicated routes through his own home, or on the part of the house, which was designed in a way that made convoluted routes unavoidable while traversing it.

[6b] which is why the specific anatomy of these routes has been omitted.

[7] I have a final theory on these panels I was hesitant to share earlier: they are preludes to Kellan's disappearance, moments in which he was still here but already gone, gaps in his existence, as if he vanished out of time between the last finished panel before the blank ones and the first finished panel after them so that it was the moments of creation themselves, the complex symbiosis between Kellan and Reality, that

were erased. Certainly, it is the hardest to grasp of my theories, the most outrageous, but also the one I am most unable to let go.

[8] The images in this panel and the ones that immediately follow it are sized so that the entirety of the worms fits into the view (i.e., the worms are the baseline, compared to which the man seems small), though the perspective is not one, such as an aerial, that would explain this. It is more like a viewing from a distance, one that would be normally impossible as the man's house would be in the way.

[9] I needed the glasses to see this as the man's speech bubble was reduced in size like everything else.

[10] I presume this to be the one that was seen eating the earlier versions of the golem and continue with this presumption going forward.

[11] I needed the glasses here as well.

[12] The sizing here returns to what it had been previously in this issue (i.e., is now such that the man is the baseline and the worms seem large) and then varies going forward. At no other point in this issue are any of the man's actions rendered at a scale that makes them difficult to decipher.

Cover: Looking down on the grassy field from far up in the sky, the hole visible as a circle with the circumference of a pencil's eraser, what's in the hole obscured by the distance.

Summary:

The man's backyard, still torn up. The sun, not visible in the panel, is above the horizon somewhere, providing morning light to the scene. Several panels of this view, centered around the hole the man dropped into in the previous issue[2]. A bird flies into the scene, lands on the ground at the edge of the hole, pecks the ground once, flies off. Then a hand emerges from within the hole and grabs the edge. The man pulls himself from the hole. He is covered in dirt[3].

The dirt covered man in his study. He picks the paper off his desk, crumples it, and throws it in a garbage can next to the desk. He begins to walk away, but something occurs to him. He turns around and retrieves the note from the garbage.

The dirt covered man in the backyard again. The man throws the crumpled page into the hole.

The man in the shower. The dirt on him thick and red. What washes off runs in trails like blood down his body into the drain. What clings to him clings as a heavy mud. He makes no effort to scrub it off; the water from the showerhead—which he stands beneath like someone might stand beneath a waterfall, an exhausted stand beneath the water–does the work. It slowly melts the mud from his body. As it melts away, the mud and the man have a conversation[4]. "You can't stay," says the mud. "She's not safe." "Where are we going to go?" says the man. "You know where," says the mud. "I can't," says the man. "You have to," says the mud. "You have to." "I don't know how," says the man. "You have to for her," says the mud. "I need a little time," says the man. "More lemons?" says the mud. The man laughs. "What do I tell her?" he says. "That it's time to go," says the mud. "Will she be happy there?" says the man. "Go," says the mud, as the last of it melts away. "Go now."

The man, dressed, his hair still wet, sits down on the edge of the bed next to where the golem still sleeps. He places a hand on her shoulder and shakes her gently. The golem's eyes open. "Daddy?" she says. "Yes," says the man. "It's me." "Are they back?" says the golem. "Did the big worms come back?" "Not yet," says the man. "But they will. So we're going to take a little trip." "A trip to where?" says the golem. "Some place safe," says the man. "But we need to go now. It's a long trip. I need you to wake up and pack your things. Ok?" "I packed them yesterday," says the golem. "That's right," says the man. "I forgot. I guess I just need you to wake up and get dressed." "Can I have breakfast?" says the golem. "I'm hungry." "Ok," says the man. "We will have breakfast and then we will go."

The man sits at the dining room table. Across from him sits the golem. Between them: a box of Marshmallow Ka-Pows. Before them: two bowls. They eat. Suddenly, the golem stops eating and looks up at the man. "Daddy?" she says. "Yes," says the man. "Are you going to pack the stories?" says the golem. "Of course," says the man. He puts his spoon down. "You finish eating. I have to do something. Then we'll go." "Ok," says the golem. The man stands from the table and leaves the kitchen.

The man tours the house. In the living room, he stops in front of the TV unit. He picks up the snow globe and looks into it. He shakes it and looks into it again. He puts it down. Then he's in the study. He pulls some pages out of one of his desk drawers, folds them, and puts them in the back pocket of his pants. He pulls a new sheet of paper out of a different drawer and puts it on the desktop. He picks up a pen and writes something on the paper. Then he's in one of the bathrooms, looking at himself in the mirror. Then he's in the golem's bedroom, tracing the outline of Moosipher with his index finger. Then he's in the backyard, pressing his hand into the trunk of a tree. Then he's in the master bedroom, opening the chest of the grandfather clock. He puts an ornate brass key into a slot inside the clock's internal mechanisms and begins to turn. He turns the key over and over, panel after panel for two full pages, the panels shrinking in size as he does this so that the second and third panels occupy the space that would have been occupied by the second panel alone had it been the size of the first, so that the fourth, fifth and sixth panels occupy the space that would have been occupied by the third panel alone had it been the size of the first, so that the seventh, eighth, ninth, and tenth panels occupy the space that would have been occupied by the fourth panel alone had it been the size of the first, etc...[5]

The man returns to the kitchen. "Are you ready?" he says to the golem. The golem nods. She gets up from her chair. The man places a sheet of paper on the table, near the bowl he was eating from. He turns to the golem and takes her hand. They leave the room. The final few panels of the issue contain only the table and the bowls sitting on top of it. The perspective slowly moves in on them until the paper that the man left on the table is visible. It's another note. It reads:

To whom it may concern:

This house is yours now. Don't worry about winding the clock. I have wound it to outlive whatever grief will befall you[6].

Notes

____

[1] I swear that when I looked in the mirror this morning, I saw Kellan. It wasn't a fleeting moment. I looked into the mirror and there was Kellan looking back at me. I closed my eyes and opened them again and there was Kellan looking back at me. Egret mentioned grief again and pointed me toward something that Marcio LeBernadine, the food critic in *Brine Comedy,* says in his review of Verunica's restaurant after he eats there during the climax of Vernuica's breakdown. "The grief mind is capable of anything," he writes. "In the culinary world, to bake something is to rationalize it, to set the logic of it into form. The grief mind is perfectly unbaked."

[2] It is easy here to imagine the morning stillness.

[3] It is my understanding that Jeremy Stronk, who has received an advanced copy of this book, is currently at work on an essay that attempts to dissect the hole in the story here, the literal hole (the absence of any detail about what happened to the man in the hole, whether it was some sort of hellquest or a confrontation with the Legions or just him meditating in the dark of the hole), and the figurative one (the hole itself that the Legion has created).

[4] It took me a few moments to understand this was happening. It is clear that a conversation is taking place, but I could not figure out who the second party was. First, I thought the golem was in the bathroom, outside the view, but the speech bubble indicated the speech was coming from something in the shower. Then I thought the man was talking to himself, since the speech bubbles pointed the words toward the middle of his body (where the stubborn mud had collected in a clump), but the other speech bubbles pointed directly toward his mouth and I couldn't make sense of why only one of the two sets of speech bubbles would point to the man's mouth if he was talking to himself[4a]. I finally surrendered to the uncanny option and accepted that it was the mud itself that was speaking to him, which, given what this series is about, makes sense.

[4a] In the past, Kellan has used dueling, mouth-pointing speech bubbles when a character is speaking to himself, such as the lengthy "dialogue"

in *Mytosis* between Quaalude and Quaalude that occurs after Quaalude, for the second of three times, consumes the titular drug that causes the user to hallucinate a doppelganger, an exchange Kellan decided to present from the perspective of a non-omniscient on-looker (in contrast to the scenes containing the first and third times he takes the drug, where the perspective is from within the hallucinatory state).

[5] Just like in Issue 10, the images become impossibly small here but maintain their coherence (as best as I could tell using the glasses before the images became so small that they were blurry owing to the limitations of my eyes).

[6] I have debated with myself whether or not I correctly remembered the order in which the man did the things he does before they leave, specifically whether he wrote the note about the clock before winding it or if he wound the clock first. I do think that he wrote the note first and then wound the clock, which is strange.

Issue 21

Cover: A photograph of the man, now old and gray, standing next to an adult female golem adorned in a larger pair of window-framed glasses, the two of them in front of a beautiful castle, the man holding a mug that says world's best dad, the golem pointing to the mug while kissing the man on the cheek.

Summary:

The first page is completely white except for this centered epigraph:

"There is salt in my soul."
-Robot 0111000101[1]

Then:

Aerial view of an ocean, no land in site, a small boat is visible. Zoom in: the man and the golem on a white rowboat equipped with a short mast. The man is rowing. The golem leans over the side of the boat, looking into the water. "I think I saw another one," says the golem. "Do they ever come out of the water?" "Some of them do," says the man. "Some of them will jump out of the water and bite your nose off." "No they won't," says the golem. "You're making that up." "Am not," says the man. "Some of them, their favorite thing to eat is little girls' noses." The golem leans back from the water slowly. Then she moves quickly to the center of the boat, in front of the man and the oars. "I'm going to talk to the birds with my mind," says the golem.

Pan out: the boat visible from about ten feet away, from a perspective near the surface of the water. Several gulls are floating on the wind over the boat. The golem stares at them. Over the course of several panels a thought bubble forms, starting with the smallest connector bubble, the one nearest to the golem's head, followed by the next smallest, followed by the largest connector bubble, followed finally by the main bubble itself, which encases the birds in the thought. The golem then grabs the smallest connector bubble and hoists herself up onto it. She uses the other two connector bubbles as steps and climbs into the thought bubble with the birds. Once inside, she hoists herself on to the lowest flying bird and proceeds to step up along the birds to the highest flying, which is flying near the top of the thought bubble. At this point, half the golem is in the thought bubble and half the golem, from the waist up, is beyond the bubble's top edge. "I love the birds, Daddy," says the golem. "I know you do," says the man.

The view shifts into the boat, toward the man. He stops rowing, pulls the oars into the boat, and carefully stands up. He turns to the mast behind him. He finds a cord and pulls on it, raising a sail. The sail catches wind, and the man sits back down. The golem is back in the boat.

For a page worth of panels, rendered at various distances from the boat, also from various angles (above, to the side, looking across the boat from stern to bow, from below[2], etc....), the man and the golem sail the unchanging ocean[3].

The focus returns to the man and the golem in the center of the boat. "Daddy," says the golem, "read me that part from that story again. The one that I really like." "Ok," says the man. He reaches into the hull of the boat and pulls up a backpack. He opens the backpack, rifles through it, and pulls out several pages. He closes the backpack and puts it back on the floor of the boat. The golem claps her hands in excitement. "Read it good," she says. "Ok," says the man.

The man begins to read: "'I don't believe that the world and reality are the same thing,' said Ruck. 'Why then do you care so much about crushing one flower?' asked Lara. 'Because the dream of life still has meaning, and if you crush all the flowers without feeling grief, that meaning sours,' said Ruck. 'But you only crushed one flower,' said Lara. 'But if I don't grieve, I have crushed them all,' said Ruck."

The man puts the pages down. "Daddy," says the golem, "do I feel grief?" "Grief for what?" says the man. "I don't know," says the golem. "I just want to know if I feel it." "I can't answer that," says the man. "But if you do feel grief someday, I promise that you'll know it." The golem nods and leans toward the side of the boat, looking over the edge into the water. View from just behind the window frame glasses, looking through them at the water: the reflection of the golem looks up from the water's surface, the glasses absent from its face, what appears to be a slim twinkle of light slipping from its left eye, glazing the galaxy mark on its cheek[4].

The golem leans back fully into the boat and faces the man, who is now looking at a compass that he holds in his hands. "Daddy," says the golem, "what's reality?" The man continues to look at the compass. "What's that?" he says. "What's reality?" says the golem. The man looks up. "Well," says the man, "It's kind of complicated. It's the one thing that belongs to everyone, and at the same time, it's also the most deeply personal thing there is." The man pauses in thought. "But I don't think that really explains it," he continues. The man brings the compass next to his ear and shakes it. "Let's see," he continues, "Maybe we can say that reality is the milk that the…" He pauses. "No," he says, "that's not good. Maybe it's…" He pauses again. "Maybe," he says, "I'm not the best person to ask. I'm not sure that I know." The golem stands up and walks towards the man. She puts her hand on his shoulder. "That's ok, Daddy," she says. "You don't have to know everything." The golem's eyes grow wide with awe behind the glasses. "Maybe the fish know," she says. She darts to the side of the boat and leans her head over again. Several distorted fish forms are visible through the water's surface. A thought bubble forms from the golem like it did earlier in the issue, piece by piece, this time toward the water, the final part of it forming beneath the surface, encasing three bright, rainbow-colored fish. Where before the golem stepped her way up to the thought bubble until she was in it with the birds, now she squeezes herself into each of the smaller lead-up bubbles, one after another, until she is inside the bubble with the fish. "Do you know what reality is?" the golem says. The fish turn and stare at her. One of them approaches her face. Close-up: the head of the fish an inch or so away from the girl's nose.

Back in the boat, the man continues to study the compass. He stops and checks the sail. He puts the compass in the backpack. He takes out some pages and a clipboard. He starts to write. The shot zooms out, the perspective gaining elevation, looking down on the boat from directly above it: the entire boat is visible, the man alone in it, and around it the ocean, in which something floats beneath the surface, obscured by refraction. Further outward zoom: the boat, still visible as a boat (the man a speck), on the ocean, surrounded by water. Further zoom: the boat a white speck, surrounded by ocean. Further zoom: the boat a black dot, ocean and ocean and ocean, but at the panels edge, the beginning of a land mass. Further zoom: the boat too small to see, a mass of land surrounded by the ocean, a city at its center. Zoom: the land mass, surrounded by ocean, the city now a grayish speck in the middle. Zoom: the land mass now a yellowish speck in a field of blue ocean. Zoom: a field of blue ocean. And then another field. Then another. Then another.

Pages and pages and pages of ocean[5].

Notes

---

[1] One of the characters from *A Conspiracy of Slumber*, though this quote is not from that work, nor do robots in that work speak in such poetic terms.

[2] The world above, the sun and the boat bottom and the birds, and the head of the golem as it peeks out again over the side of the boat, refracted through the water.

[3] The ocean does change panel to panel, but in ways that are meaningless to a person interested in the larger story (someone focused, for instance, on the destination and the pair's distance from it, of which information this scene contains none)[3a].

[3a] Kellan, I am certain, went to great lengths to portray the subtle movements of the ocean, as he did in *Harpoon Follies*; although in that work, he includes a scene in which Ahab, while naming each distinct wave that he sees after Mobitha, describes the complexity of each ocean moment in an encyclopedic fashion, the types of waves, their personalities, their emotional states, etc... Here there is only silence, perhaps to allow the ocean's complexity to speak for itself.

[4] Wherever the actual manuscript is now, there is a teardrop on this panel of it.

[5] I know that Kellan, after completing *Harpoon Follies*, had expressed a desire to tell a story entirely through the ocean's rolling. Maybe this is that story or part of it.

Blackfoot
A man seeks forgiveness for stepping on a rare flower.

Brine Comedy
A chef in search of a flavor experienced in a dream descends into madness while running the kitchen of a famous restaurant.

Clothespins and Circuses
The story of Madge McGuinty, a member of a freakshow that tours a futuristic utopia in which everyone is beautiful and perfect, whose freak defect is that she is unable to control the dreams she has.

A Conspiracy of Slumber
In an idyllic future, robots ponder how their creation, having robbed their creators of the need to do anything for themselves, led to humanity's decline and eventual extinction.

Crustacean Wedding
Marco, Marjorie, and Matthew, three individuals in their early 30s, subsume themselves in a bizarre love triangle.

Cupcakes

A young, slightly autistic gay man bakes cupcakes as a means to connect with the other people in his small town.

D.ynamo O.pera S.ynergy

Inspired by the works of ancient Greece, D.ynamo O.pera S.ynergy is the story of the epic, love-soaked war between the techno-mythological kingdoms of Farce and Province.

The Digit

A man known only as 1 is trapped alone in a room where he is observed, as part of an experiment, by some never-seen presence known only as The Overseer.

Harpoon Follies

A reimagining of *Moby Dick* in which an old sea captain named Ahab rides around on a giant white whale named Richard, with whom he battles a variety of sea monsters as he attempts to win the heart of a woman named Mobitha.

I, Angel

An angel comes to earth, curious about the taste of human flesh.

The Mall Beasts

A group of janitors and support staff working in secret build and then move into a tunnel system under the mall where they work.

Maze on Dixon

At a neighborhood coffee shop, Seraphim, a man from Kenya, and Maryanne, a woman from Ireland, discuss the past, present and future of Superland, the country in which they live.

Mytosis

A new drug appears on the streets of Orchard Parish, unraveling the hundreds of years of order that have been kept by four powerful families.

Punching Bag

A past-his-prime boxer finds work as a sparring partner for up-and-coming talent.

Ratio of Sanity

A sexless person named Otello seeks a way to produce offspring in a world governed by strict codes of conduct.

Static If

When the sun stops setting in Morton, a vigilante culture arises to combat the erratic behaviors that begin to plague the city.

Tramplemundus

The story of three super-powered individuals–The Edge Perfect, Polygon Two and Lullaby–whose alter-egos all, unbeknownst to each other, work for the Munduson company, where the idiotic daily grind gradually diminishes their desires to use their abilities for good.

Windmill Betty

A documentarian follows a group of artists who've been challenged to create a piece of art that viewers will prefer over a single episode of a hit TV show.

About the Author

Philip Jason's stories can be found in magazines such as Prairie Schooner, The Pinch, Mid-American Review, Ninth Letter, and J Journal; his poetry in Spillway, Lake Effect, Canary and Summerset Review. He is a recipient of the Henfield Prize in Fiction. His first collection of poetry, *I Don't Understand Why It's Crazy to Hear the Beautiful Songs of Nonexistent Birds*, is available from Fernwood Press. For more information, visit philipjason.com, where you can also find some of the music he has made.

Phil would like to thank Jen, Julia and Jil for their considerable help, support and contributions.

About the Press

Unsolicited Press is based out of Portland, Oregon and focuses on the works of the unsung and underrepresented. As a womxn-owned, all-volunteer small publisher that doesn't worry about profits as much as championing exceptional literature, we have the privilege of partnering with authors skirting the fringes of the lit world. We've worked with emerging and award-winning authors such as Shann Ray, Amy Shimshon-Santo, Brook Bhagat, Kris Amos, and John W. Bateman.

Learn more at unsolicitedpress.com. Find us on twitter and instagram.

www.ingramcontent.com/pod-product-compliance
Lightning Source LLC
Chambersburg PA
CBHW061446210726
48287CB00007B/2376